Kingdoms™

A Biblical Epic

The Prophet's Oracle

The Prophet's Oracle

Requests for information should be addressed to:

Zondervan, *Grand Rapids, Michigan 49530*

Library of Congress Cataloging-in-Publication Data

Avery, Ben, 1974–
The prophet's oracle / story by Ben Avery; art by Mat Broome; created by Brett Burner.
p. cm. -- (Kingdoms: a Biblical epic; bk. 3)
ISBN-13: 978-0-310-71355-5 (softcover)
ISBN-10: 0-310-71355-2 (softcover)
1. Graphic novels. I. Broome, Mat. II. Burner, Brett A., 1969- III. Title
PN6727.A945P76 2008
741.5'973--dc22

2007030925

This book published in conjunction with Lamp Post, Inc.; 8367 Lemon Avenue, La Mesa, CA 91941

Series Editor: Bud Rogers
Managing Editor: Bruce Nuffer
Managing Art Director: Sarah Molegraaf

Printed in the United States of America

08 09 10 11 12 13 • 23 22 21 20 19 18 17 16 15 14 13 12 11 10 9 8 7 6 5 4 3 2 1

Kingdoms™

A Biblical Epic

The Prophet's Oracle

Series Editor: Bud Rogers
Story by Ben Avery
Art by Mat Broome
Created by Brett Burner

ZONDERVAN.com/
AUTHORTRACKER
follow your favorite authors

CHAPTER ONE

"The Calling of the Weeping Prophet"

In the days of Josiah, there lived a man in the town of Anathoth.
A man named Jeremiah.
A priest, he had dedicated his life to following the Lord and teaching people about the Lord's ways.
Little did he know, upon joining the priesthood, that his calling would go quite a bit further than serving one small town.
JEREMIAH.
WHO'S THERE?

BEFORE I FORMED YOU IN THE WOMB I KNEW YOU.

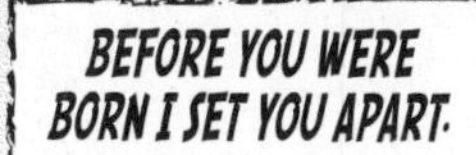
BEFORE YOU WERE BORN I SET YOU APART.

I APPOINTED YOU AS A PROPHET TO THE NATIONS.
A PROPHET?!

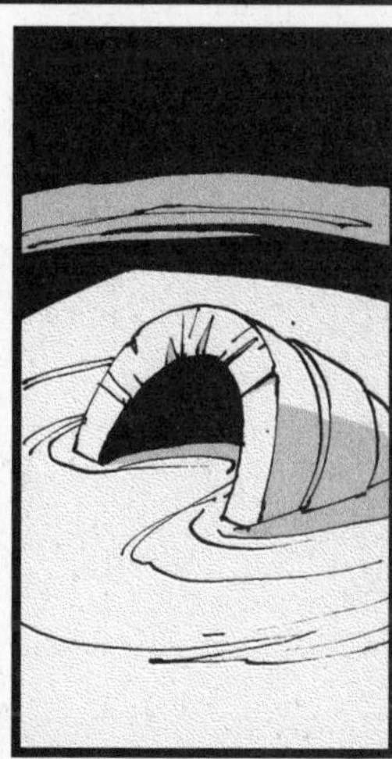

LORD, I ...

I DO NOT KNOW HOW TO SPEAK; I AM ONLY A CHILD.

DO NOT SAY, "I AM ONLY A CHILD." YOU MUST GO TO EVERYONE I SEND YOU TO AND SAY WHATEVER I COMMAND YOU. DO NOT BE AFRAID OF THEM, FOR I AM WITH YOU AND WILL RESCUE YOU.

SEE!

WHAT ...

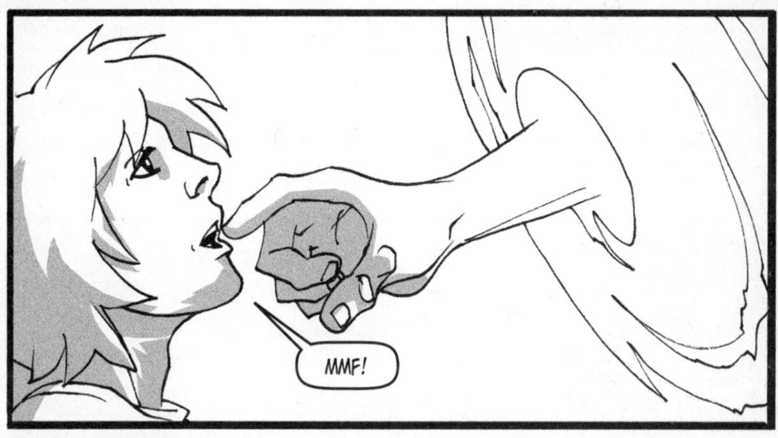
MMF!

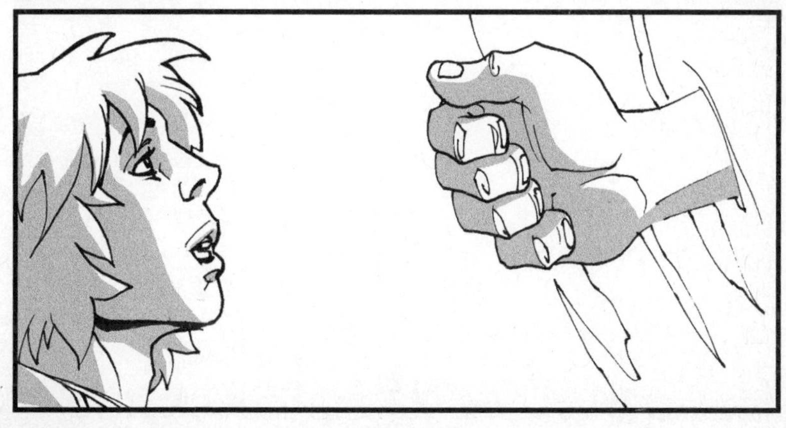

NOW, I HAVE PUT MY WORDS IN YOUR MOUTH.
SEE, TODAY I APPOINT YOU OVER NATIONS AND KINGDOMS TO UPROOT AND TEAR DOWN, TO DESTROY AND OVERTHROW, TO BUILD AND TO PLANT.

FROM THE NORTH DISASTER WILL BE POURED OUT ON ALL WHO LIVE IN THE LAND.
I WILL PRONOUNCE MY JUDGMENTS ON MY PEOPLE BECAUSE OF THEIR WICKEDNESS IN FORSAKING ME, IN BURNING INCENSE TO OTHER GODS AND IN WORSHIPING WHAT THEIR HANDS HAVE MADE.

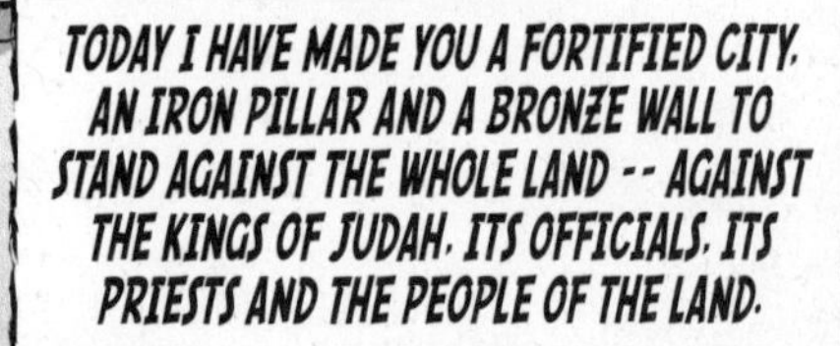
GET YOURSELF READY! STAND UP AND SAY TO THEM WHATEVER I COMMAND YOU.
TODAY I HAVE MADE YOU A FORTIFIED CITY, AN IRON PILLAR AND A BRONZE WALL TO STAND AGAINST THE WHOLE LAND -- AGAINST THE KINGS OF JUDAH, ITS OFFICIALS, ITS PRIESTS AND THE PEOPLE OF THE LAND.

THEY WILL FIGHT AGAINST YOU BUT WILL NOT OVERCOME YOU, FOR I AM WITH YOU AND WILL RESCUE YOU.

I HAVE TO LEAVE.
I HAVE TO GO TO JERUSALEM.
WHY? WHAT OF YOUR DUTIES HERE?
MY FIRST DUTIES ARE TO THE LORD. AND TO THE PEOPLE OF HIS NATION.
SOMETHING HAS HAPPENED, SON ... TELL ME MORE.

I M NOT SURE I CAN.

TRY ME.
THIS IS GOING TO SOUND LIKE SOME FORM OF MADNESS.
I HAVE HEARD THE WORD OF GOD.

HIS VOICE! HE SPOKE! AND I HEARD!
HE TOUCHED ME!!!

I M TO GO TO JERUSALEM TO BE GOD S VOICE THERE!
HE HAS MESSAGES FOR THE PEOPLE OF HIS NATION! AND HE WISHES TO SPEAK THROUGH ME!

IT WAS ALMOST LIKE MOSES!
I EVEN TOLD HIM I WASN T A GOOD SPEAKER -- I MEAN, I WASN T THINKING OF MOSES WHEN I SAID IT, BUT --

TEACHER. WHAT IS WRONG?

I CAN ASSURE YOU, THIS **WAS** HIS VOICE!

I DO NOT DOUBT THAT.

WALK WITH ME, SON.

TEACHER, I PROMISE YOU, IT WAS GOD WHO SPOKE TO ME.
THAT IS NOT WHAT CAUSES ME CONCERN.

I WANT TO TELL YOU A STORY.
A STORY YOU HAVE ALREADY HEARD.
BUT YOU NEED TO BE REMINDED.

YEARS AGO, IN THE DAYS OF THE REIGN OF SAUL, THERE WAS A PRIEST.
HIS NAME WAS ABIATHAR.
I KNOW THIS STORY ...
HUSH.
LISTEN.

"KING SAUL HAD BEEN LOOKING FOR DAVID, WHO HAD BEEN PROMISED THE THRONE THROUGH GOD'S SPEAKER SAMUEL, BUT HE HAD BEEN UNSUCCESSFUL.
"DAVID HAD BECOME THE PEOPLE'S HERO IN MANY WAYS; SAUL HAD LOST THE PEOPLE'S TRUST.
"SAUL WANTED TO RETAIN THE CROWN, PASS IT TO HIS SON.
DAVID HAS BECOME THE PEOPLE'S HERO.
BUT I ASK YOU, WILL HE GIVE YOU FIELDS? VINEYARDS?
WILL HE MAKE YOU COMMANDERS AND GENERALS?

WHAT CAN HE GIVE YOU THAT WOULD CAUSE YOU TO CONSPIRE AGAINST ME?
FOR THAT IS WHAT IS HAPPENING.
MY OWN SON MAKES A COVENANT WITH THE SON OF JESSE, AND NONE OF YOU TELL ME.
DAVID WAITS FOR ME, AND NONE OF YOU ARE CONCERNED ABOUT ME.

WE ARE BROTHERS -- ALL FROM THE TRIBE OF BENJAMIN.
HRM ...

DAVID IS OF THE TRIBE OF JUDAH.
BUT THESE THINGS MEAN NOTHING TO YOU, DO THEY?

DO THEY!?!

YOU MAY AS WELL TAKE THE CROWN FROM MY BROW YOURSELVES!
GO ON!
TAKE IT!
IT'S WHAT YOU WANT!

TAKE IT!
GIVE IT TO THAT PRETENDER TO THE THRONE, DAVID!
GO ON!

HRM?
HAVE YOU NOTHING TO SAY?

YOU ARE FOOLS!

SIRE ...
THERE IS SOMETHING YOU SHOULD KNOW.

I SAW DAVID.
IN NOB.
HE CAME TO AHIMELECH, SON OF AHITUB, THE PRIEST THERE IN NOB.
AHIMELECH INQUIRED OF THE LORD FOR DAVID ... AND GAVE HIM PROVISIONS AND THE SWORD OF GOLIATH THE PHILISTINE, THE GIANT SLAIN BY THE HAND OF DAVID --

I KNOW WHO GOLIATH IS!
YOU NEED NOT REMIND ME!

BRING THE PRIEST TO ME.

"AHIMELECH WAS BROUGHT TO KING SAUL.
MY KING, WHAT MAY I DO FOR YOU?
DO NOT PATRONIZE ME, PRIEST.
WHY DO YOU CONSPIRE AGAINST ME WITH DAVID?

YOU GIVE HIM A SWORD. FOOD. AND PRAYER.
NOW, HE IS WAITING FOR ME OUT THERE -- ARMED AND RESTED. BECAUSE OF YOU. READY TO SEIZE MY CROWN.
WHY?

MY KING, DAVID IS YOUR SERVANT.
YOUR SON-IN-LAW.
YOUR WARRIOR.
HE HAS BEEN A GUEST IN YOUR HOUSE, HIGHLY RESPECTED.
I HAVE ALWAYS INQUIRED OF THE LORD FOR HIM, YOUR SERVANT.
I KNOW NOTHING ABOUT WHAT YOU SPEAK.

HMMMM.

KILL HIM.
...

HE IS A MAN OF GOD!
WE CANNOT STRIKE DOWN ONE SUCH AS HIM!
WHAT IS KING SAUL SAYING?

KILL HIM, AND THEN GO TO NOB AND KILL ALL THE PRIESTS THERE.
THEY HAVE SIDED WITH DAVID.
THEY ALL KNEW HE WAS FLEEING, BUT THEY DID NOT TELL ME.
SO THEY DIE AS WELL.

HRM.

YOU.
KILL HIM.
THEN TAKE THOSE OF MY PEOPLE WHO HAVE NOT BECOME COWARDS AND GO STRIKE THE REST OF THEM DOWN.

"EIGHTY-FIVE MEN WHO WORE THE LINEN EPHOD WERE KILLED THAT DAY.
"MANY IN THE TOWN OF NOB -- MEN, WOMEN, AND CHILDREN -- WERE DESTROYED.
"SOME OF THESE WERE DESCENDANTS OF THE PRIEST ELI, AND THIS FULFILLED THE PROPHECY SAMUEL PRONOUNCED AGAINST ELI ABOUT THE OLD PRIEST'S FAMILY.

DAVID!
DAVID!

WHO ... WHAT IS THAT PRIEST HERE FOR?

KING SAUL! HE IS MAD!
MAD!

WHAT DO YOU MEAN?
WHAT HAS HAPPENED?
KING SAUL HAS PUT TO THE SPEAR THE PRIESTS ... ONLY I ESCAPED ... NOB IS DEAD!

NO.
I AM SORRY.
THIS IS BECAUSE OF ME.

PLEASE. STAY WITH ME.
THE MAN WHO SEEKS TO TAKE YOUR LIFE ALSO SEEKS TO TAKE MY OWN.
YOU WILL BE SAFE WITH ME.

"LATER, DURING THE DAYS OF THE REIGN OF DAVID, DAVID FACED A THREAT TO HIS OWN THRONE IN THE FORM OF HIS OWN SON.
"ABSALOM WAGED A CIVIL WAR AGAINST KING DAVID, AND KING DAVID WAS ONCE MORE ON THE RUN.
"ABIATHAR AND ANOTHER PRIEST, ZADOK, STOOD AT KING DAVID'S SIDE.
MY SON HAS TAKEN MY THRONE FOR THE TIME BEING.

THE THRONE IS NOT HIS.
BUT I CANNOT FIGHT HIM NOW. THE HEARTS OF ISRAEL ARE WITH HIM.
AND SO EVEN THOUGH I AM THE RIGHTFUL KING, THE ARK OF THE COVENANT DOES NOT BELONG WITH ME.

IT BELONGS IN THE CAPITAL CITY.
ZADOK. ABIATHAR. YOU HAVE BOTH SERVED GOD AND ME FAITHFULLY.
GO. TAKE YOUR SONS. RETURN THE ARK TO JERUSALEM.

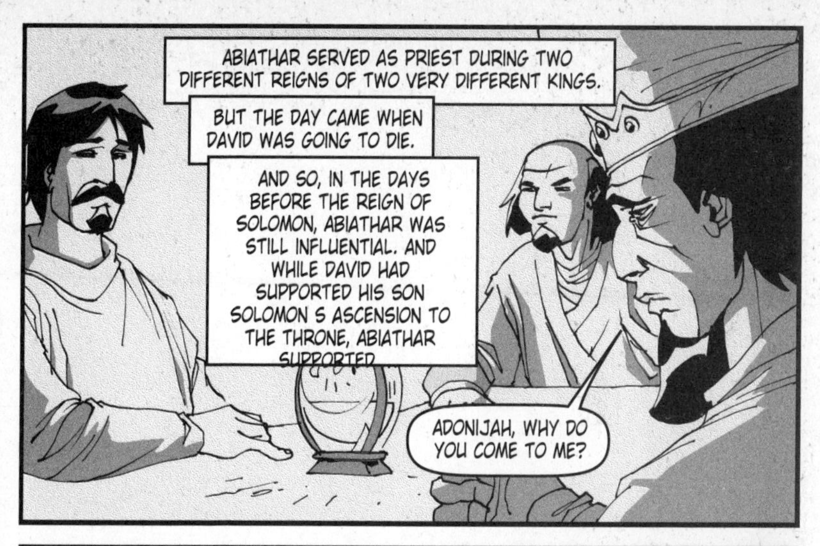
ABIATHAR SERVED AS PRIEST DURING TWO DIFFERENT REIGNS OF TWO VERY DIFFERENT KINGS.
BUT THE DAY CAME WHEN DAVID WAS GOING TO DIE.
AND SO, IN THE DAYS BEFORE THE REIGN OF SOLOMON, ABIATHAR WAS STILL INFLUENTIAL. AND WHILE DAVID HAD SUPPORTED HIS SON SOLOMON S ASCENSION TO THE THRONE, ABIATHAR SUPPORTED
ADONIJAH, WHY DO YOU COME TO ME?

I WANT TO BE KING.
WITH DAVID S HIGHEST WAR COMMANDER AND PRIEST ON MY SIDE, I WILL GET WHAT I WANT.
ARE YOU WITH ME?
HM ... YOU ARE OF THE BLOODLINE ...

YES.
WE WILL GIVE YOU OUR SUPPORT.

SOLOMON, OF COURSE, WAS CROWNED.
AND THEREFORE ...

ABIATHAR, YOU SUPPORTED ADONIJAH IN HIS BID FOR THE THRONE THAT WAS RIGHTFULLY MINE.
BUT ADONIJAH HAS BEEN DEALT WITH. SEVERELY. HE NO LONGER WALKS THIS EARTH.
THE LORD HAS ESTABLISHED A DYNASTY, ABIATHAR. AS I SIT ON MY FATHER'S THRONE, I AM THE NEXT IN THAT DYNASTY. AND MY SON WILL FOLLOW ME.
ZADOK SUPPORTS ME. BUT YOU?
YOU DO NOT SUPPORT THE DYNASTY AND SOUGHT TO PUT ANOTHER IN THIS PLACE.

ABIATHAR, YOU SERVED MY GOD AND MY FATHER.
BUT YOU HAVE NOT SERVED ME.
NOR SHALL YOU.

YOU DESERVE TO DIE, ALONG WITH YOUR CO-CONSPIRATORS.
GO.
GO BACK TO THE FIELDS OF ANATHOTH.
ONCE, LONG AGO, YOU ESCAPED DEATH AT THE HANDS OF KING SAUL. TODAY YOU ESCAPE DEATH AT ANOTHER KING'S HANDS.

YOU ARE NO LONGER A PRIEST!
"AND SO, THE LAST PRIEST IN THE LINE OF ELI'S PRIESTLY FAMILY WAS EXILED."

YES. EXILED TO COME HERE.
TO ANATHOTH.
WHY DO YOU TELL ME THIS STORY?
THAT GOD HAS CALLED YOU I HAVE NO DOUBTS.
BUT DO YOU KNOW WHAT THE CALLING MEANS?
IT MEANS I WILL SPEAK HIS WORDS TO THE NATION!
TO THE *NATIONS*!
YES.
IT ALSO MEANS THAT BAD THINGS ARE GOING TO COME UPON US.
JOSIAH SITS ON THE THRONE NOW, AND HE HAS DONE MUCH GOOD.
BUT THIS MEANS THAT THE CYCLE OF KINGS WHO DO EVIL IN GOD S SIGHT MIGHT BEGIN AGAIN -- IF AND WHEN JOSIAH IS TAKEN FROM US.
I CAN UNDERSTAND WHY GOD HAS CHOSEN YOU, THOUGH.
YOU ARE PASSIONATE. COMPASSIONATE. YOU LOVE HIM. YOU LOVE HIS PEOPLE.
AND YOU COME FROM ANATHOTH.
WHAT HAS THAT TO DO WITH ANYTHING?

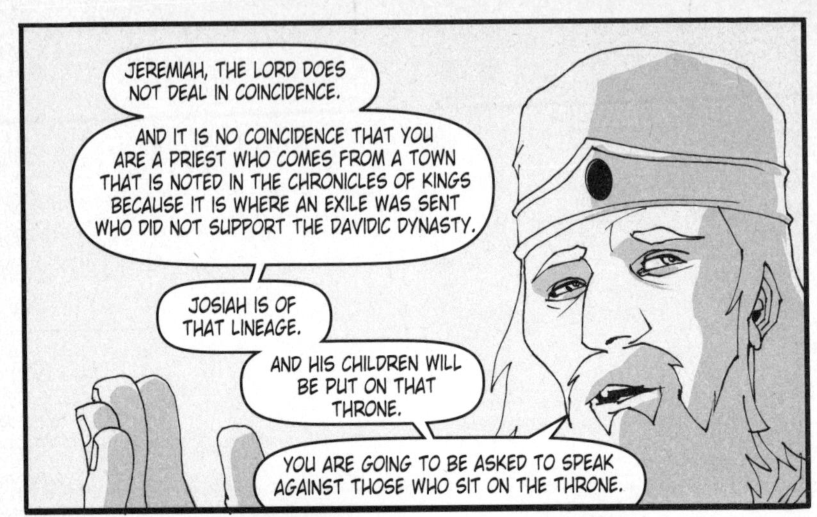
JEREMIAH, THE LORD DOES NOT DEAL IN COINCIDENCE.
AND IT IS NO COINCIDENCE THAT YOU ARE A PRIEST WHO COMES FROM A TOWN THAT IS NOTED IN THE CHRONICLES OF KINGS BECAUSE IT IS WHERE AN EXILE WAS SENT WHO DID NOT SUPPORT THE DAVIDIC DYNASTY.
JOSIAH IS OF THAT LINEAGE.
AND HIS CHILDREN WILL BE PUT ON THAT THRONE.
YOU ARE GOING TO BE ASKED TO SPEAK AGAINST THOSE WHO SIT ON THE THRONE.

YES ... HE SAID SOMETHING TO THAT EFFECT.

THOSE WHO DO NOT FOLLOW THE LORD DO NOT TAKE KINDLY TO THOSE WHO SPEAK THE LORD S WORDS ... ESPECIALLY WHEN IT IS AGAINST THEM.

And the word of the Lord came to Jeremiah:
"Go and proclaim in the hearing of Jerusalem …"
And Jeremiah followed the calling of the Lord.

Jeremiah's message continued through the end of Josiah's reign and into the reigns of Josiah's sons.
HEAR THE WORD OF THE LORD, ALL YOU PEOPLE OF JUDAH WHO COME THROUGH THESE GATES TO WORSHIP THE LORD.
THIS IS WHAT THE LORD ALMIGHTY, THE GOD OF ISRAEL, SAYS: "REFORM YOUR WAYS AND YOUR ACTIONS, AND I WILL LET YOU LIVE IN THIS PLACE.

"DO NOT TRUST IN DECEPTIVE WORDS AND SAY, 'THIS IS THE TEMPLE OF THE LORD, THE TEMPLE OF THE LORD, THE TEMPLE OF THE LORD!'

"IF YOU REALLY CHANGE YOUR WAYS AND YOUR ACTIONS AND DEAL WITH EACH OTHER JUSTLY, IF YOU DO NOT OPPRESS THE ALIEN, THE FATHERLESS OR THE WIDOW AND DO NOT SHED INNOCENT BLOOD IN THIS PLACE, AND IF YOU DO NOT FOLLOW OTHER GODS TO YOUR OWN HARM ...
"... THEN I WILL LET YOU LIVE IN THIS PLACE, IN THE LAND I GAVE YOUR FOREFATHERS FOR EVER AND EVER. BUT LOOK, YOU ARE TRUSTING IN DECEPTIVE WORDS THAT ARE WORTHLESS.
"WILL YOU STEAL AND MURDER, COMMIT ADULTERY AND PERJURY, BURN INCENSE TO BAAL AND FOLLOW OTHER GODS YOU HAVE NOT KNOWN, AND THEN COME AND STAND BEFORE ME IN THIS HOUSE, WHICH BEARS MY NAME, AND SAY, 'WE ARE SAFE' -- SAFE TO DO ALL THESE DETESTABLE THINGS?
"HAS THIS HOUSE, WHICH BEARS MY NAME, BECOME A DEN OF ROBBERS TO YOU? BUT I HAVE BEEN WATCHING!" DECLARES THE LORD.

"GO NOW TO THE PLACE IN SHILOH WHERE I FIRST MADE A DWELLING FOR MY NAME, AND SEE WHAT I DID TO IT BECAUSE OF THE WICKEDNESS OF MY PEOPLE ISRAEL.
"WHILE YOU WERE DOING ALL THESE THINGS," DECLARES THE LORD, "I SPOKE TO YOU AGAIN AND AGAIN, BUT YOU DID NOT LISTEN; I CALLED YOU, BUT YOU DID NOT ANSWER."
EXCUSE ME ... WHO IS THAT MAN?
HIM? PSH! I DO NOT KNOW, NOR DO I CARE!
"THEREFORE, WHAT I DID TO SHILOH I WILL NOW DO TO THE HOUSE THAT BEARS MY NAME, THE TEMPLE YOU TRUST IN, THE PLACE I GAVE TO YOU AND YOUR FATHERS."
WHAT CAN YOU TELL ME ABOUT HIM?
I DON'T KNOW ... NOW EXCUSE ME!

"I WILL THRUST YOU FROM MY PRESENCE, JUST AS I DID ALL YOUR BROTHERS, THE PEOPLE OF EPHRAIM."
I'M NOT SURE OF HIS NAME. JEREMIAH? JEBEDIAH? NO MATTER.
HE'S OUT HERE QUITE OFTEN, WARNING OF A THREAT FROM THE NORTH.
WARNING US TO DESTROY OUR IDOLS AND TURN BACK TO THE LORD.

"THEREFORE THIS IS WHAT THE SOVEREIGN LORD SAYS: MY ANGER AND MY WRATH WILL BE POURED OUT ON THIS PLACE ..."
STANDARD DOOM-AND-GLOOM STUFF.
NOW IF YOU'LL EXCUSE ME ...

"... ON MAN AND BEAST, ON THE TREES OF THE FIELD AND ON THE FRUIT OF THE GROUND, AND IT WILL BURN AND NOT BE QUENCHED."

MHM.

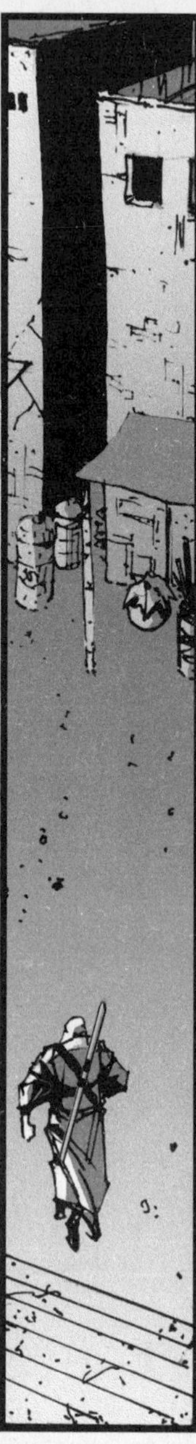

M-MHM ...

HMM.

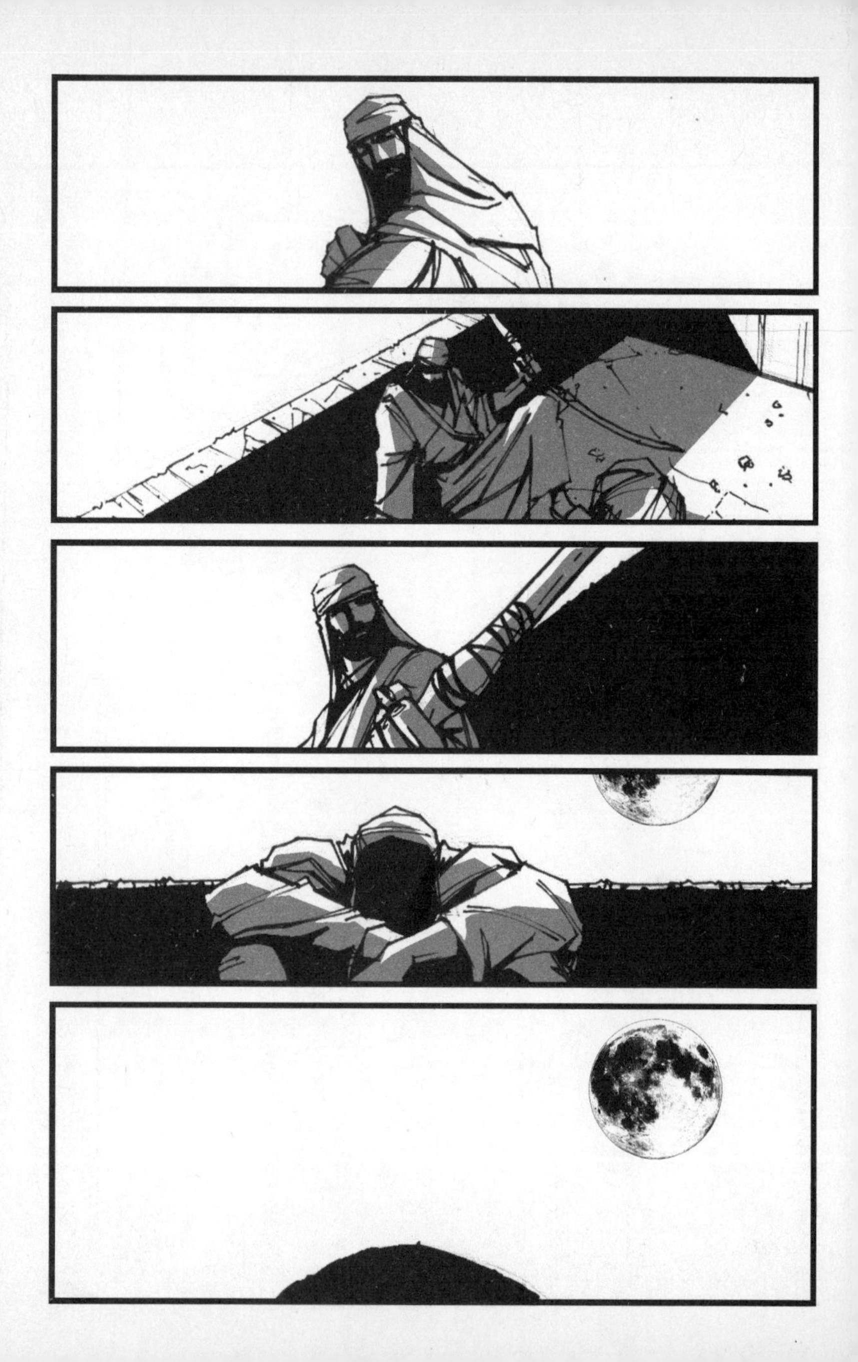

HEAR WHAT THE LORD SAYS TO YOU, O HOUSE OF ISRAEL!
"THESE GODS, WHO DID NOT MAKE THE HEAVENS AND THE EARTH, WILL PERISH FROM THE EARTH AND FROM UNDER THE HEAVENS."
BUT GOD MADE THE EARTH BY HIS POWER; HE FOUNDED THE WORLD BY HIS WISDOM AND STRETCHED OUT THE HEAVENS BY HIS UNDERSTANDING.
WHEN HE THUNDERS, THE WATERS IN THE HEAVENS ROAR!

HE MAKES CLOUDS RISE FROM THE ENDS OF THE EARTH!
HE SENDS LIGHTNING WITH THE RAIN AND BRINGS OUT THE WIND FROM HIS STOREHOUSES.
EVERYONE IS SENSELESS AND WITHOUT KNOWLEDGE; EVERY GOLDSMITH IS SHAMED BY HIS IDOLS.
HIS IMAGES ARE A FRAUD; THEY HAVE NO BREATH IN THEM.
THEY ARE WORTHLESS, THE OBJECTS OF MOCKERY; WHEN THEIR JUDGMENT COMES, THEY WILL PERISH.
PTUEW!!!
HE WHO IS THE PORTION OF JACOB IS NOT LIKE THESE!
FOR HE IS THE MAKER OF ALL THINGS!

INCLUDING ISRAEL, THE TRIBE OF HIS INHERITANCE --
THE LORD ALMIGHTY IS HIS NAME!
GATHER UP YOUR BELONGINGS TO LEAVE THE LAND, YOU WHO LIVE UNDER SIEGE.
FOR THIS IS WHAT THE LORD SAYS: "AT THIS TIME I WILL HURL OUT THOSE WHO LIVE IN THIS LAND; I WILL BRING DISTRESS ON THEM SO THAT THEY MAY BE CAPTURED."
LISTEN!
THE REPORT IS COMING --

A GREAT COMMOTION FROM THE LAND OF THE NORTH!
IT WILL MAKE THE TOWNS OF JUDAH DESOLATE ...
A HAUNT OF JACKALS!

WHA--
HUH?

IMPOSSIBLE!
WHO ...?

WHO'S THERE?

GASP!

JEREMIAH, YOU MUST UNDERSTAND!

JEREMIAH ... TO BRING THE MONARCHY'S ATTENTION TO ANATHOTH ... WITH OUR HISTORY OF GOING AGAINST THE MONARCHY ...
THE MESSAGES YOU BROUGHT TO THE PEOPLE ...
THEY WERE NOT POPULAR MESSAGES!
THIS IS NOT ABOUT POPULARITY.
THIS IS ABOUT TRUTH.
THE "TRUTH," AS YOU CALL IT, COULD BRING RUIN TO US!
KILLING ME WILL NOT STOP THE TRUTH.
THE LORD REVEALS HIS TRUTH TO ME.
HE HAS REVEALED TRUTHS ABOUT THE *NATIONS*. ABOUT *JUDAH*.
ABOUT YOU.

THE LORD TOLD ME OF YOUR PLOT.
HOW YOU PLANNED TO "DESTROY THE TREE AND ITS FRUIT."
"CUT JEREMIAH OFF FROM THE LAND OF THE LIVING, THAT HIS NAME BE REMEMBERED NO MORE."
THE LORD TOLD ME OF YOUR FATE.
"I WILL PUNISH THEM," HE TOLD ME.
"THEIR YOUNG MEN WILL DIE BY THE SWORD, THEIR SONS AND DAUGHTERS BY FAMINE.
"NOT EVEN A REMNANT WILL BE LEFT OF THEM, BECAUSE I WILL BRING DISASTER ON THE MEN OF ANATHOTH IN THE YEAR OF THEIR PUNISHMENT."
RUIN WILL COME TO YOU, NOT BECAUSE THE MONARCHY WILL BE UNHAPPY WITH MY MESSAGE -- AND NO DOUBT IT WILL BE.
RUIN WILL COME TO YOU BECAUSE THE LORD IS UNHAPPY WITH YOUR COWARDLY, FOOLISH ACTION AGAINST HIS ANOINTED.

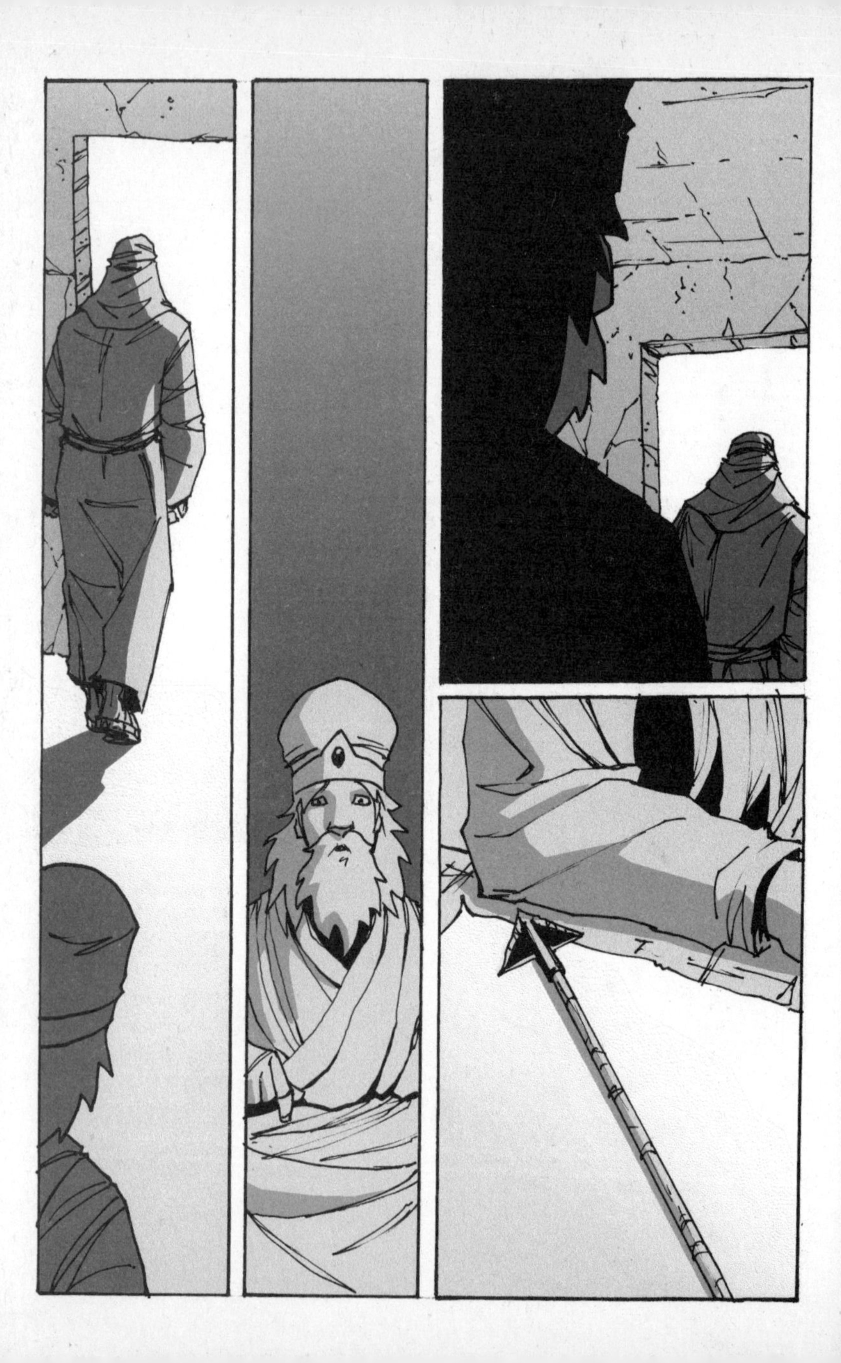

CHAPTER TWO

"Two Baskets of Figs"

After the reign of King Josiah, his sons took the throne in quick succession.
Jehoahaz, son of Josiah, reigned for three months. He did evil in the eyes of the Lord and was taken captive into Egypt by Pharaoh Neco, where he died.

Jehoiakim, son of Josiah, reigned for eleven years. He did evil in the eyes of the Lord and was taken captive into Babylon by King Nebuchadnezzer.
IDDO! SHAPHAN!
WE'VE EXPECTED YOU.
Jehoiachin, son of Jehoiakim, reigned for three months and ten days. He did evil in the eyes of the Lord and surrendered to King Nebuchadnezzer.

HELLO, BARUCH.
Nebuchadnezzer stripped the Lord's temple of all items of value and deported ten thousand of Jerusalem's fighting men, artisans, and leaders to Babylon, while placing Mattaniah on the throne.

PLEASE, SIT.
Nebuchadnezzer changed Mattaniah's name to Zedekiah. Zedekiah, son of Josiah, was twenty-one years old when he became king.

He did evil in the eyes of the Lord …
JEREMIAH?

WELCOME, IDDO.
WELCOME, SHAPHAN.
IT HAS BEEN TOO LONG.

WE WERE IN EGYPT.
WE JUST RETURNED A FEW WEEKS AGO.
I'M SORRY YOU HAD TO RETURN TO ...

... THIS.

I MISSED AN ENTIRE REIGN.
ONE KING SENDS US TO PARLEY A DEAL WITH THE EGYPTIANS FOR PROTECTION, AND WE RETURN HOME ONLY TO FIND THAT A SECOND KING ALREADY SURRENDERED HIMSELF TO THE BABYLONIANS AND A THIRD KING IS NOW ON THE THRONE!
YES, NOW MATTANIAH IS KING --

NO.
HIS NAME IS NOW ZEDEKIAH.

HIS BABYLONIAN NAME.
WHY DO THEY INSIST ON FORCING THEIR NAMES ON US?
IT GIVES THEM CONTROL.
IDDO, I AM SORRY ABOUT WHAT HAPPENED TO YOUR FAMILY.
IT WAS A TERRIBLE PURGING. THEY TOOK ANYTHING AND ANYONE OF VALUE, LEAVING JERUSALEM ESSENTIALLY LEADERLESS EXCEPT FOR A PUPPET KING.
WHEN JOSIAH WAS KING, I NEVER IMAGINED ANYTHING LIKE THIS WOULD HAPPEN.
EVEN WHEN JOSIAH WAS KING, THE LORD TOLD US OF THIS DAY.

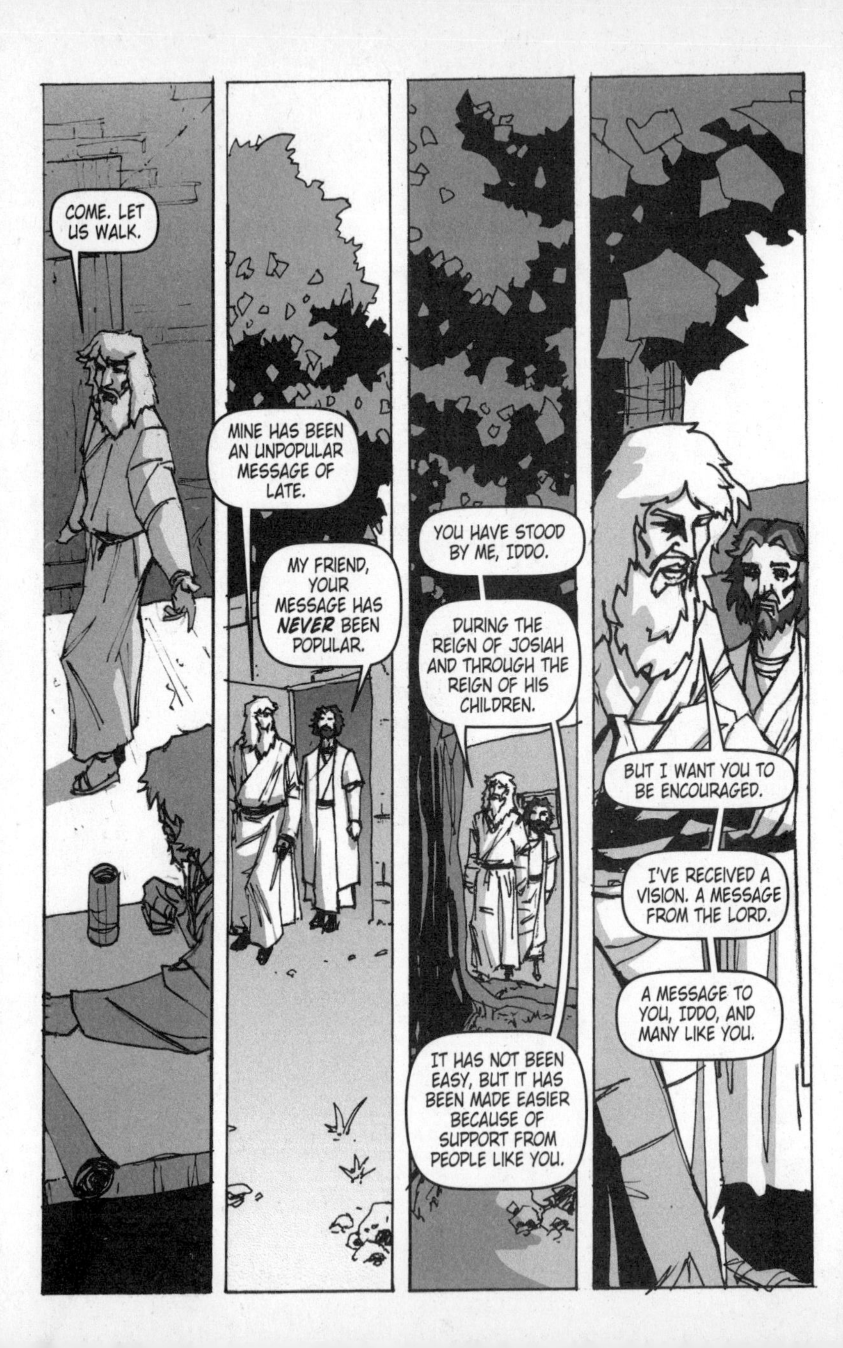
COME. LET US WALK.
MINE HAS BEEN AN UNPOPULAR MESSAGE OF LATE.
MY FRIEND, YOUR MESSAGE HAS *NEVER* BEEN POPULAR.
YOU HAVE STOOD BY ME, IDDO.
DURING THE REIGN OF JOSIAH AND THROUGH THE REIGN OF HIS CHILDREN.
IT HAS NOT BEEN EASY, BUT IT HAS BEEN MADE EASIER BECAUSE OF SUPPORT FROM PEOPLE LIKE YOU.
BUT I WANT YOU TO BE ENCOURAGED.
I'VE RECEIVED A VISION. A MESSAGE FROM THE LORD.
A MESSAGE TO YOU, IDDO, AND MANY LIKE YOU.

THE LORD SHOWED ME TWO BASKETS OF FIGS PLACED IN FRONT OF THE TEMPLE OF THE LORD.
ONE BASKET HAD VERY GOOD FIGS, LIKE THOSE THAT RIPEN EARLY.
THE OTHER BASKET HAD VERY POOR FIGS, SO BAD THEY COULD NOT BE EATEN.
THEN THE LORD ASKED ME,
WHAT DO YOU SEE, JEREMIAH?
FIGS.
THE GOOD ONES ARE VERY GOOD.
THE POOR ONES ARE SO BAD THEY CANNOT BE EATEN.

THEN THE WORD OF THE LORD CAME TO ME:
LIKE THESE GOOD FIGS, I REGARD AS GOOD THE EXILES FROM JUDAH, WHOM I SENT AWAY FROM THIS PLACE TO THE LAND OF THE BABYLONIANS.
MY EYES WILL WATCH OVER THEM FOR THEIR GOOD, AND I WILL BRING THEM BACK TO THIS LAND.
I WILL BUILD THEM UP AND NOT TEAR THEM DOWN; I WILL PLANT THEM AND NOT UPROOT THEM.
I WILL GIVE THEM A HEART TO KNOW ME, THAT I AM THE LORD.
THEY WILL BE MY PEOPLE, AND I WILL BE THEIR GOD, FOR THEY WILL RETURN TO ME WITH ALL THEIR HEART.

BUT THE POOR FIGS, WHICH ARE SO BAD THEY CANNOT BE EATEN, SO I WILL DEAL WITH ZEDEKIAH KING OF JUDAH, HIS OFFICIALS, AND THE SURVIVORS FROM JERUSALEM, WHETHER THEY REMAIN IN THE LAND OR LIVE IN EGYPT.
I WILL MAKE THEM ABHORRENT AND AN OFFENSE TO ALL THE KINGDOMS OF THE EARTH, A REPROACH AND A BYWORD, AN OBJECT OF RIDICULE AND CURSING, WHEREVER I BANISH THEM.
I WILL SEND THE SWORD, FAMINE, AND PLAGUE AGAINST THEM UNTIL THEY ARE DESTROYED FROM THE LAND I GAVE THEM AND THEIR FATHERS.

JEREMIAH.

AM I TO BELIEVE THAT MY FAMILY IS SAFER IN BABYLON THAN HERE?

IT WOULD SEEM SO.

COME, JEREMIAH.
WHAT IS NEXT?

NEXT?
WELL, I KNOW WHAT'S NEXT FOR ME, MY FRIEND.

AH, HELLO ... GEDALIAH, IS IT?
YES. MY GRANDSON.
TO WHAT DO I OWE THE PLEASURE OF YOUR VISIT?

JEREMIAH, I KNOW I'M ABOUT TO SPEAK TO YOU OF SOMETHING YOU ARE ALREADY AWARE.
BUT IN CASE YOU AREN'T, I WANTED TO BRING YOU THESE TIDINGS.

IT HAS BEEN MERE WEEKS SINCE THE BABYLONIANS HAVE TAKEN SO MUCH FROM US ...
ALREADY, PROPHETS HAVE BEGUN SPEAKING ABOUT OUR PEOPLE.

ALL CONTEND THEY SPEAK THE LORD'S WORDS.
BUT THERE ARE SOME OF US WHO AWAIT YOUR WORDS.
BECAUSE WE KNOW YOUR WORDS TRULY ARE THE LORD'S WORDS.
PLEASE, JEREMIAH ...

I BEG OF YOU.
BREAK YOUR SILENCE AND BRING THE LORD'S WORDS TO OUR PEOPLE.
WE NEED IT NOW MORE THAN EVER ...

YOU HAVE THE LORD'S WORDS.
I'VE SPOKEN THEM OVER THE YEARS, NUMEROUS TIMES.
MANY OF THOSE WORDS REFER TO THIS TIME THAT HAS COME UPON US.

WHEN THE LORD GIVES ME A NEW MESSAGE FOR YOU, YOU WILL KNOW.
TRUST ME.

JEREMIAH, THANK YOU ...
GEDALIAH, JEREMIAH TOLD ME OF A VISION HE HAD ...
WAS HIS VISION OF THE EXILES RETURNING HOME?
NO, BUT THEY WILL BE SAFE ...
GET SOME INK AND A SCROLL, BARUCH.
WE HAVE A LETTER TO WRITE.

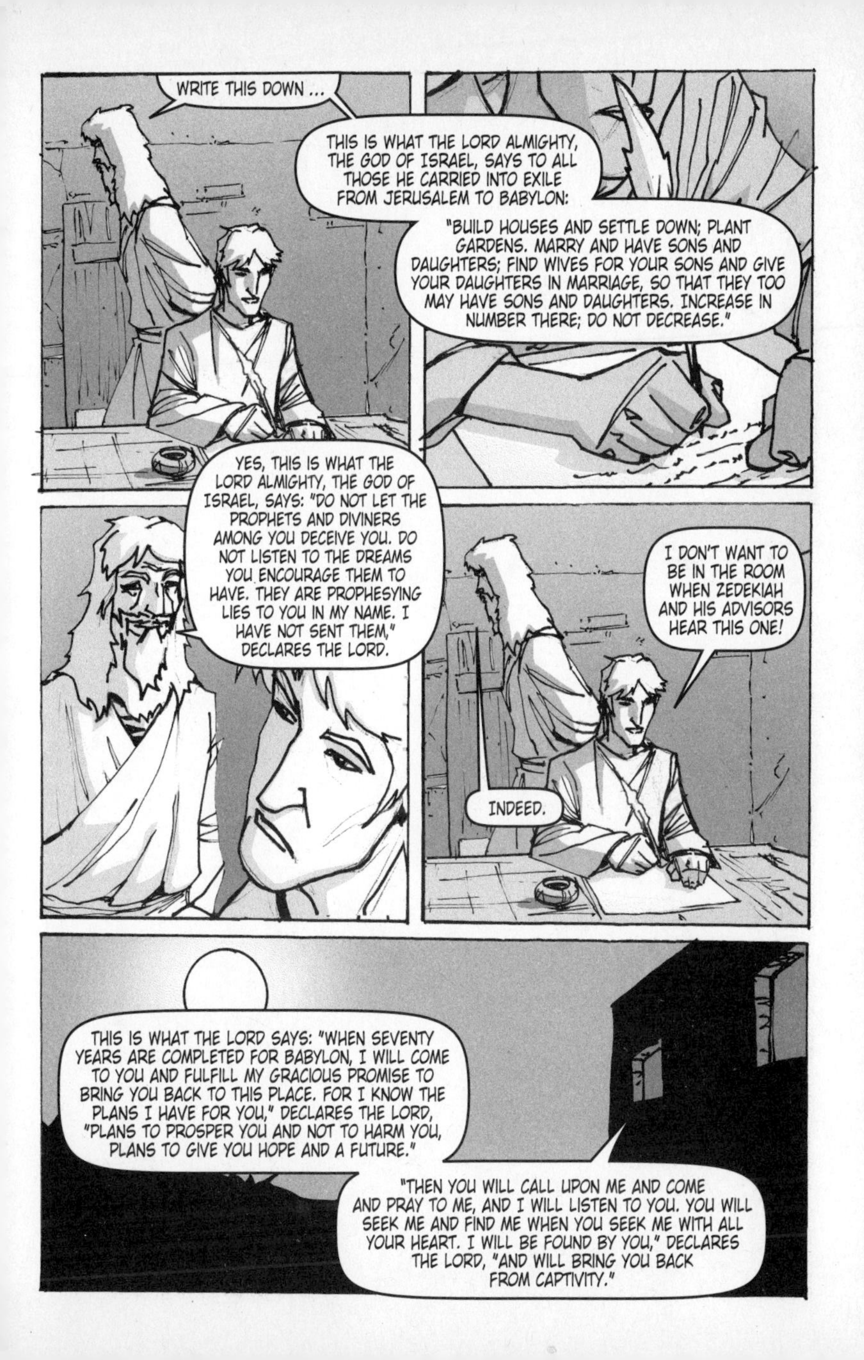
WRITE THIS DOWN ...
THIS IS WHAT THE LORD ALMIGHTY, THE GOD OF ISRAEL, SAYS TO ALL THOSE HE CARRIED INTO EXILE FROM JERUSALEM TO BABYLON:
"BUILD HOUSES AND SETTLE DOWN; PLANT GARDENS. MARRY AND HAVE SONS AND DAUGHTERS; FIND WIVES FOR YOUR SONS AND GIVE YOUR DAUGHTERS IN MARRIAGE, SO THAT THEY TOO MAY HAVE SONS AND DAUGHTERS. INCREASE IN NUMBER THERE; DO NOT DECREASE."
YES, THIS IS WHAT THE LORD ALMIGHTY, THE GOD OF ISRAEL, SAYS: "DO NOT LET THE PROPHETS AND DIVINERS AMONG YOU DECEIVE YOU. DO NOT LISTEN TO THE DREAMS YOU ENCOURAGE THEM TO HAVE. THEY ARE PROPHESYING LIES TO YOU IN MY NAME. I HAVE NOT SENT THEM," DECLARES THE LORD.
I DON'T WANT TO BE IN THE ROOM WHEN ZEDEKIAH AND HIS ADVISORS HEAR THIS ONE!
INDEED.
THIS IS WHAT THE LORD SAYS: "WHEN SEVENTY YEARS ARE COMPLETED FOR BABYLON, I WILL COME TO YOU AND FULFILL MY GRACIOUS PROMISE TO BRING YOU BACK TO THIS PLACE. FOR I KNOW THE PLANS I HAVE FOR YOU," DECLARES THE LORD, "PLANS TO PROSPER YOU AND NOT TO HARM YOU, PLANS TO GIVE YOU HOPE AND A FUTURE."
"THEN YOU WILL CALL UPON ME AND COME AND PRAY TO ME, AND I WILL LISTEN TO YOU. YOU WILL SEEK ME AND FIND ME WHEN YOU SEEK ME WITH ALL YOUR HEART. I WILL BE FOUND BY YOU," DECLARES THE LORD, "AND WILL BRING YOU BACK FROM CAPTIVITY."

SHAPHAN? GEDELIAH?
I THOUGHT YOU WOULD LIKE TO SEE THIS.
I COPIED IT MYSELF FROM ANOTHER COPY THAT HAS BEEN PASSED AROUND.

JEREMIAH HAS FINALLY SPOKEN, AND IT DOES NOT SOUND GOOD.

HAS ANYONE ELSE SPOKEN OUT ABOUT THIS?
THE OTHER PROPHETS?

YES. THEY HAVE.
ALMOST TO A PERSON, THEY DENOUNCE JEREMIAH'S WORDS.

WHICH IS WHAT INCLINES ME TO BELIEVE THAT THIS IS A MESSAGE FROM THE LORD.

HM.
THIS LETTER ... IT IS GOOD ... AND BAD ...

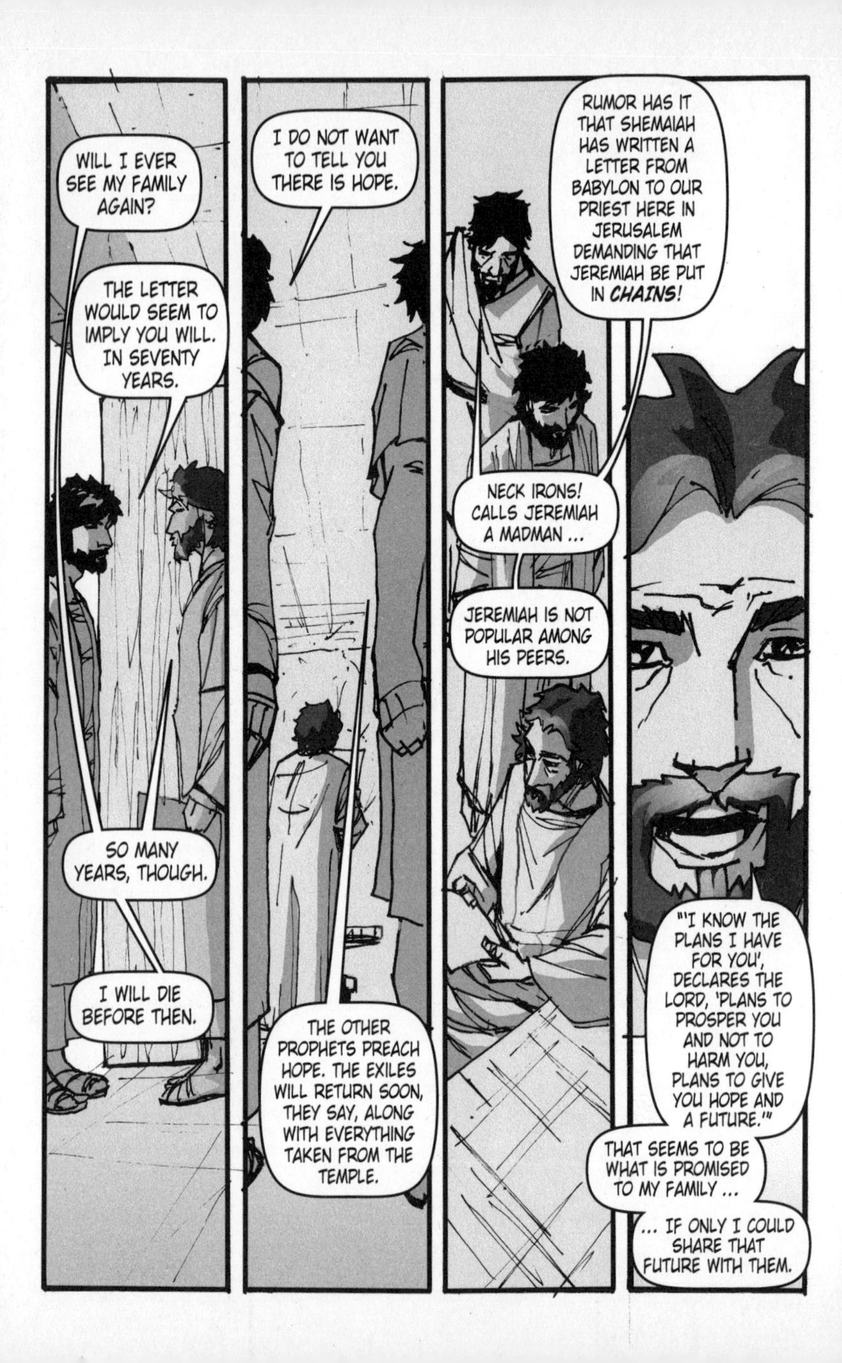
WILL I EVER SEE MY FAMILY AGAIN?
THE LETTER WOULD SEEM TO IMPLY YOU WILL. IN SEVENTY YEARS.
SO MANY YEARS, THOUGH.
I WILL DIE BEFORE THEN.
I DO NOT WANT TO TELL YOU THERE IS HOPE.
THE OTHER PROPHETS PREACH HOPE. THE EXILES WILL RETURN SOON, THEY SAY, ALONG WITH EVERYTHING TAKEN FROM THE TEMPLE.
RUMOR HAS IT THAT SHEMAIAH HAS WRITTEN A LETTER FROM BABYLON TO OUR PRIEST HERE IN JERUSALEM DEMANDING THAT JEREMIAH BE PUT IN CHAINS!
NECK IRONS! CALLS JEREMIAH A MADMAN ...
JEREMIAH IS NOT POPULAR AMONG HIS PEERS.
"'I KNOW THE PLANS I HAVE FOR YOU', DECLARES THE LORD, 'PLANS TO PROSPER YOU AND NOT TO HARM YOU, PLANS TO GIVE YOU HOPE AND A FUTURE.'"
THAT SEEMS TO BE WHAT IS PROMISED TO MY FAMILY ...
... IF ONLY I COULD SHARE THAT FUTURE WITH THEM.

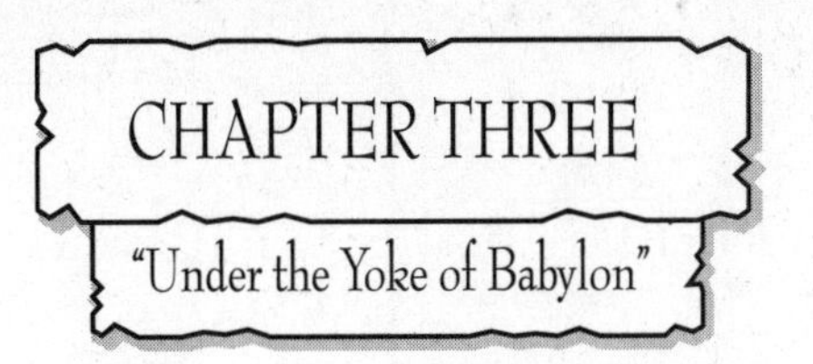
CHAPTER THREE
"Under the Yoke of Babylon"

Early in the reign of Zedekiah, son of Josiah king of Judah, this word came to Jeremiah from the Lord:
THE LORD SAYS, WITH MY GREAT POWER AND OUTSTRETCHED ARM I MADE THE EARTH AND ITS PEOPLE AND THE ANIMALS THAT ARE ON IT, AND I GIVE IT TO ANYONE I PLEASE.
NOW I WILL HAND ALL YOUR COUNTRIES OVER TO MY SERVANT NEBUCHADNEZZAR KING OF BABYLON.
ALL NATIONS WILL SERVE HIM AND HIS SON AND HIS GRANDSON UNTIL THE TIME FOR HIS LAND COMES; THEN MANY NATIONS AND GREAT KINGS WILL SUBJUGATE HIM.
IF, HOWEVER, ANY NATION OR KINGDOM WILL NOT SERVE NEBUCHADNEZZAR KING OF BABYLON OR BOW ITS NECK UNDER HIS YOKE, I WILL PUNISH THAT NATION WITH THE SWORD, FAMINE AND PLAGUE, UNTIL I DESTROY IT BY HIS HAND.
SO DO NOT LISTEN TO YOUR PROPHETS, YOUR DIVINERS, YOUR INTERPRETERS OF DREAMS, YOUR MEDIUMS OR YOUR SORCERERS WHO TELL YOU, YOU WILL NOT SERVE THE KING OF BABYLON.
THEY PROPHESY LIES TO YOU THAT WILL ONLY SERVE TO REMOVE YOU FAR FROM YOUR LANDS; I WILL BANISH YOU AND YOU WILL PERISH.
BUT IF ANY NATION WILL BOW ITS NECK UNDER THE YOKE OF THE KING OF BABYLON AND SERVE HIM, I WILL LET THAT NATION REMAIN IN ITS OWN LAND TO TILL IT AND TO LIVE THERE, DECLARES THE LORD.

THIS IS WHAT THE LORD SAYS: DO NOT LISTEN TO THE PROPHETS WHO SAY, "VERY SOON NOW THE ARTICLES FROM THE LORD'S HOUSE WILL BE BROUGHT BACK FROM BABYLON." THEY ARE PROPHESYING LIES TO YOU!
DO NOT LISTEN TO THEM!

IF THEY ARE PROPHETS AND HAVE THE WORD OF THE LORD, LET THEM PLEAD WITH THE LORD ALMIGHTY THAT THE FURNISHINGS REMAINING IN THE HOUSE OF THE LORD AND IN THE PALACE OF THE KING OF JUDAH AND IN JERUSALEM NOT BE TAKEN TO BABYLON!
FOR THIS IS WHAT THE LORD ALMIGHTY SAYS ABOUT THE THINGS THAT ARE LEFT IN THE HOUSE OF THE LORD AND IN THE PALACE OF THE KING OF JUDAH AND IN JERUSALEM:
"THEY WILL BE TAKEN TO BABYLON AND THERE THEY WILL REMAIN UNTIL THE DAY I COME FOR THEM," DECLARES THE LORD. "THEN I WILL BRING THEM BACK AND RESTORE THEM TO THIS PLACE."

NO!
THIS IS WHAT THE LORD SAYS TO *ME*!

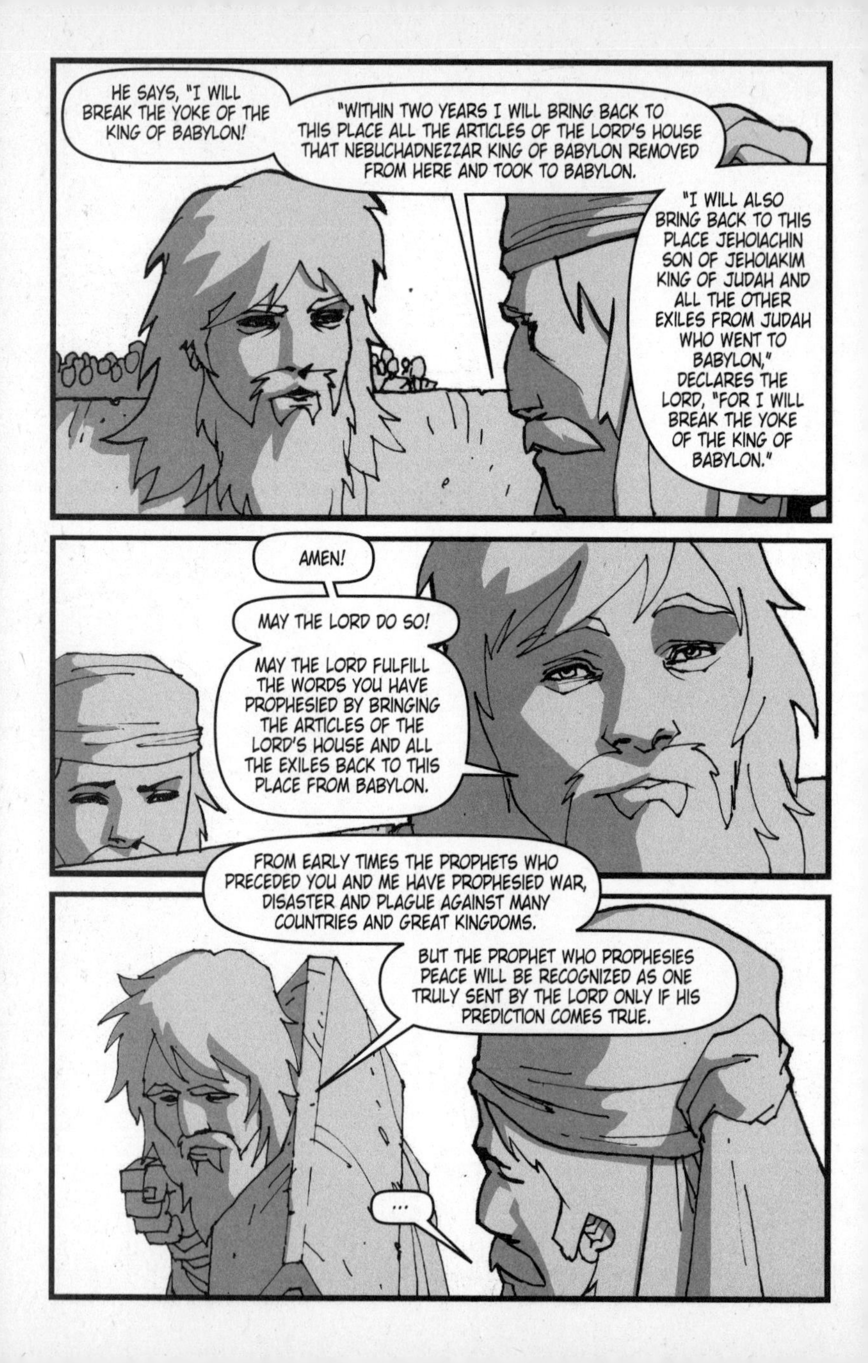
HE SAYS, "I WILL BREAK THE YOKE OF THE KING OF BABYLON!
"WITHIN TWO YEARS I WILL BRING BACK TO THIS PLACE ALL THE ARTICLES OF THE LORD'S HOUSE THAT NEBUCHADNEZZAR KING OF BABYLON REMOVED FROM HERE AND TOOK TO BABYLON.
"I WILL ALSO BRING BACK TO THIS PLACE JEHOIACHIN SON OF JEHOIAKIM KING OF JUDAH AND ALL THE OTHER EXILES FROM JUDAH WHO WENT TO BABYLON," DECLARES THE LORD, "FOR I WILL BREAK THE YOKE OF THE KING OF BABYLON."
AMEN!
MAY THE LORD DO SO!
MAY THE LORD FULFILL THE WORDS YOU HAVE PROPHESIED BY BRINGING THE ARTICLES OF THE LORD'S HOUSE AND ALL THE EXILES BACK TO THIS PLACE FROM BABYLON.
FROM EARLY TIMES THE PROPHETS WHO PRECEDED YOU AND ME HAVE PROPHESIED WAR, DISASTER AND PLAGUE AGAINST MANY COUNTRIES AND GREAT KINGDOMS.
BUT THE PROPHET WHO PROPHESIES PEACE WILL BE RECOGNIZED AS ONE TRULY SENT BY THE LORD ONLY IF HIS PREDICTION COMES TRUE.
...

AARRRHAH!!!
HUHN?
RRRGHH!!!

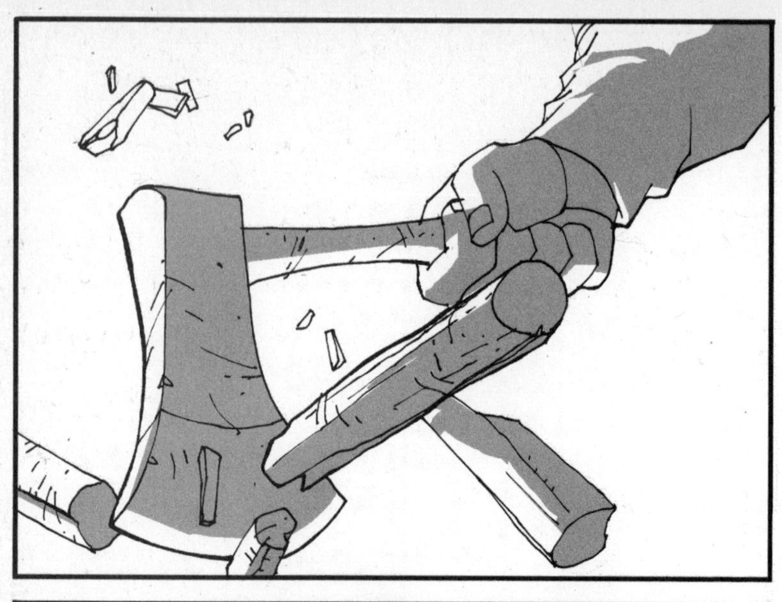

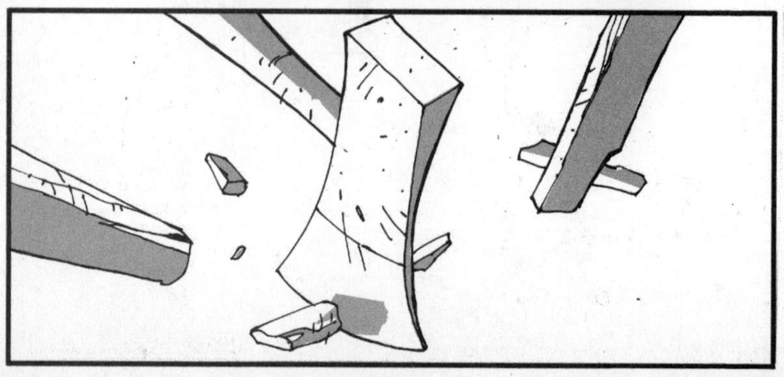

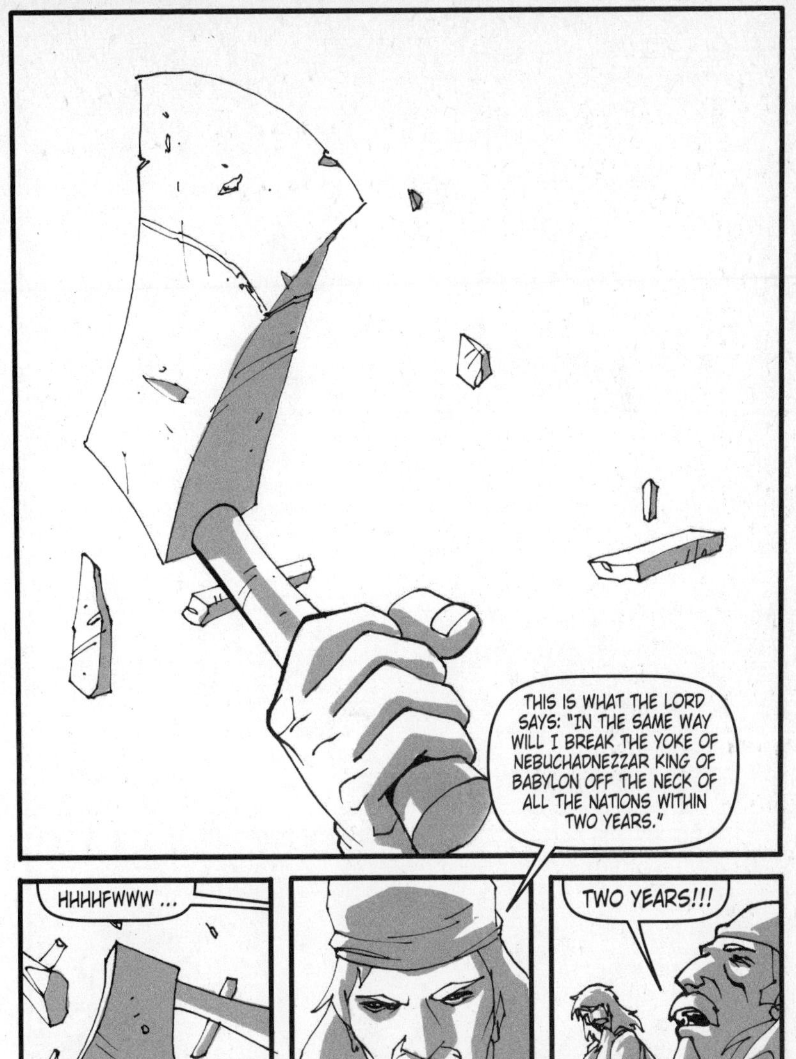
THIS IS WHAT THE LORD SAYS: "IN THE SAME WAY WILL I BREAK THE YOKE OF NEBUCHADNEZZAR KING OF BABYLON OFF THE NECK OF ALL THE NATIONS WITHIN TWO YEARS."

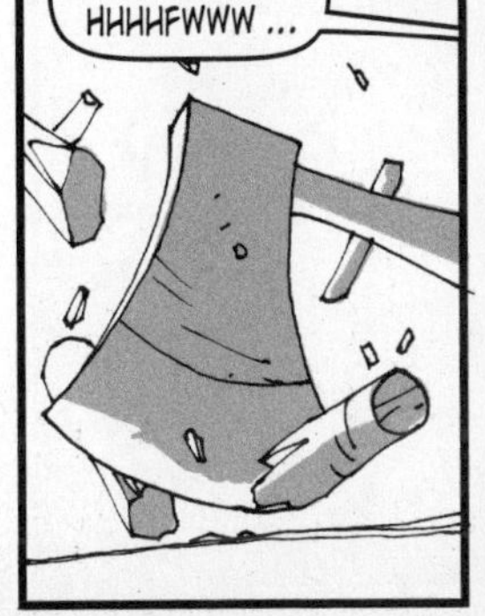
HHHHFWWW ...

TWO YEARS!!!

JEREMIAH?
THE BLIND FOLLOW THE BLIND ...
WHAT?
NEVER MIND.

JEREMIAH, IT'S KING ZEDEKIAH.
THE RUMOR IS HE'S NOT TOO HAPPY WITH YOU.
THERE ARE MANY FACTIONS WHO ARE NOT HAPPY WITH YOU.

WHAT ELSE IS NEW?
THEY WANT YOU DEAD.
IT'S BEEN TRIED.
DIDN'T WORK OUT TOO WELL FOR THEM.

THIS IS NO LAUGHING MATTER!
IDDO, DO I REALLY NEED YOU TO REMIND ME OF THAT?
I'M SORRY.
YOUR MESSAGE, THOUGH.
SURRENDER?

IT'S WHAT GOD TOLD ME TO SAY.
AND THAT'S THE ONLY REASON I'M WITH YOU ON THIS.

WHERE ARE YOU GOING?
I HAVE A MESSAGE TO DELIVER.

... THE YOKE WILL BE BROKEN IN TWO YEARS.
HANANIAH!
I'VE GOT SOME WORDS FOR YOU.
LISTEN!
REALLY!
THIS SHOULD BE GOOD!
THIS IS WHAT THE LORD SAYS: "YOU HAVE BROKEN A WOODEN YOKE, BUT IN ITS PLACE YOU WILL GET A YOKE OF IRON."
THIS IS WHAT THE LORD ALMIGHTY, THE GOD OF ISRAEL, SAYS: "I WILL PUT AN IRON YOKE ON THE NECKS OF ALL THESE NATIONS TO MAKE THEM SERVE NEBUCHADNEZZAR KING OF BABYLON, AND THEY WILL SERVE HIM. I WILL EVEN GIVE HIM CONTROL OVER THE WILD ANIMALS."
CAN YOU BELIEVE THIS!
HE JUST WON'T QUIT!

LISTEN, HANANIAH!
THE LORD HAS NOT SENT YOU, YET YOU HAVE PERSUADED THIS NATION TO TRUST IN LIES.
THEREFORE, THIS IS WHAT THE LORD SAYS:
"I AM ABOUT TO REMOVE YOU FROM THE FACE OF THE EARTH. THIS VERY YEAR YOU ARE GOING TO DIE, BECAUSE YOU HAVE PREACHED REBELLION AGAINST THE LORD."
BWHAHAH!!!
FROM EARLY TIMES THE PROPHETS WHO PRECEDED YOU AND ME HAVE PROPHESIED LIFE!

BUT THE PROPHET WHO PROPHESIES DEATH WILL BE RECOGNIZED AS ONE TRULY SENT BY THE LORD ONLY IF HIS PREDICTION COMES TRUE.
HAHAHA!!!
In the seventh month of that same year, Hananiah the prophet died.

Jeremiah also sent the message of the yoke to King Zedekiah.
"BOW YOUR NECK UNDER THE YOKE OF THE KING OF BABYLON; SERVE HIM AND HIS PEOPLE, AND YOU WILL LIVE. WHY WILL YOU AND YOUR PEOPLE DIE BY THE SWORD, FAMINE AND PLAGUE WITH WHICH THE LORD HAS THREATENED ANY NATION THAT WILL NOT SERVE THE KING OF BABYLON?
"DO NOT LISTEN TO THE WORDS OF THE PROPHETS WHO SAY TO YOU, 'YOU WILL NOT SERVE THE KING OF BABYLON,' FOR THEY ARE PROPHESYING LIES TO YOU. 'I HAVE NOT SENT THEM,'DECLARES THE LORD. 'THEY ARE PROPHESYING LIES IN MY NAME. THEREFORE, I WILL BANISH YOU AND YOU WILL PERISH, BOTH YOU AND THE PROPHETS WHO PROPHESY TO YOU.'"
ALL RIGHT, I'VE LISTENED TO YOUR MASTER'S TRIPE!
NOW, LEAVE ME!

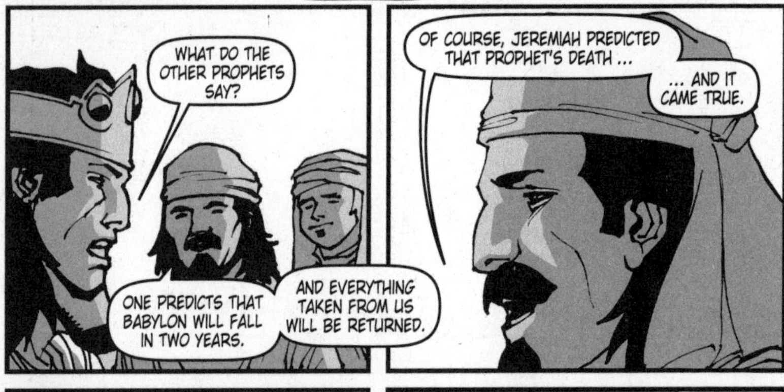
WHAT DO THE OTHER PROPHETS SAY?
ONE PREDICTS THAT BABYLON WILL FALL IN TWO YEARS.
AND EVERYTHING TAKEN FROM US WILL BE RETURNED.
OF COURSE, JEREMIAH PREDICTED THAT PROPHET'S DEATH ...
... AND IT CAME TRUE.

WHO TO BELIEVE ...
YOU HAVE TWO CHOICES, SIR.
BELIEVE THE ONE WHOSE PROPHECIES COME TRUE ...
... OR, BELIEVE THE ONE WHOSE PROPHECIES YOU LIKE.
HMMM ...

CHAPTER FOUR

"The Captivity"

The walls of Jerusalem.
AY!

YE'RE RELIEVED ...
IS IT TIME ALREADY?
YOU KNOW IT!

ANYTHING EXCITIN' HAPPEN?

YOU STILL ALIVE?
YEAH.
THEN NOTHIN' EXCITING HAPPENED.

NOPE, JUST THE SAME OLD SAME OLD.
KNOW WHAT I MEAN?

OF COURSE I KNOW ...
... WHAT ...

WHAT ARE YOU DOING?
THERE! THERE!
LOOK! LOOK!

I DON'T BELIEVE IT!
DON'T BELIEVE IT!
THEY'RE LEAVING!
THEY'RE LEAVING!
DO YOU KNOW WHAT THIS MEANS!?!

YEAH ...
... I'M GONNA LOSE MY JOB.

The home of Jeremiah, in Jerusalem.
JEREMIAH! YOU HAVE A VISITOR!
YES.

THE BABYLONIAN ARMY HAS RETREATED.
I KNOW.

I COME WITH A REQUEST FROM THE KING.
INDEED?

HIS REQUEST IS SIMPLE:
"PLEASE PRAY TO THE LORD OUR GOD FOR US."

THE BABYLONIANS RETREAT BECAUSE PHARAOH S ARMY MARCHES.
GO BACK TO THE KING AND TELL HIM THIS: PHARAOH S ARMY, WHICH HAS MARCHED OUT TO SUPPORT YOU, WILL GO BACK TO ITS OWN LAND, TO EGYPT.

THEN THE BABYLONIANS WILL RETURN AND ATTACK THIS CITY; THEY WILL CAPTURE IT AND BURN IT DOWN.
THIS IS WHAT THE LORD SAYS:
"DO NOT DECEIVE YOURSELVES, THINKING, THE BABYLONIANS WILL SURELY LEAVE US.'

"EVEN IF YOU WERE TO DEFEAT THE ENTIRE BABYLONIAN ARMY THAT IS ATTACKING YOU AND ONLY WOUNDED MEN WERE LEFT IN THEIR TENTS, THEY WOULD COME OUT AND BURN THIS CITY DOWN."

IS THAT ALL?

The Benjamin Gate of Jerusalem.
LOOK AT EVERYONE, JEREMIAH.
I'VE NOT SEEN SPIRITS SO HIGH.
THEIR HAPPINESS WILL BE SHORT LIVED.
WHERE ARE YOU GOING NOW, JEREMIAH?

I HAVE SOME FAMILY BUSINESS TO ATTEND TO; I'M GOING HOME.
I FIGURE I SHOULD USE THIS TIME TO GET IT DONE, BEFORE THE BABYLONIANS RETURN.
THEY REALLY ARE COMING BACK?

YES.
AND IF ZEDEKIAH DOES NOT COOPERATE WITH THEM, THEY WILL DESTROY THE CITY.
AND WE ALL KNOW THAT ZEDEKIAH IS NOT GOING TO COOPERATE WITH THEM.

JEREMIAH?
WHAT ARE YOU DOING HERE?

AH, CAPTAIN IRIJAH.
I AM RETURNING HOME TO ANATHOTH, WHERE I HAVE PERSONAL BUSINESS.
NO YOU AREN'T.
YES I AM.

NO.
YOU AREN'T.

I WANT TO GET THIS DONE BEFORE THE BABYLONIANS --

JEREMIAH, YOU ARE NOT LEAVING THIS CITY.
YOUR NEGATIVE FEELINGS FOR THE KING ARE WELL KNOWN, AS ARE YOUR LEANINGS TOWARD SURRENDERING THE CITY TO THE BABYLONIANS.
YOU PLAN TO DEFECT TO THE BABYLONIANS. YOU'RE ALREADY ON THEIR SIDE HERE. NOW YOU PLAN TO ACTUALLY JOIN THEM.

IRIJAH, I LOVE THIS CITY. I LOVE THIS LAND.
I ASSURE YOU, I PLAN ONLY TO TAKE CARE OF SOME PERSONAL BUSINESS AND THEN RETURN --

YOU'RE UNDER ARREST!
HOOF!!!

HE'S TELLING THE TRUTH!
STAY BACK!

WHAT IS THE CHARGE?
DEFECTION!

IT'S NOT TR --
HUHN!

SHUT UP, OLD MAN!
YOU ARE A TRAITOR AND A FOOL!
HOW DARE YOU TELL US TO SURRENDER!?!
YOU, WHO PEOPLE WILL LISTEN TO! YOU, TELLING PEOPLE TO GIVE UP! YOU, TELLING MY GUARDS TO LAY DOWN THEIR ARMS!
YOU.
MAKE.
ME.
SICK.
PTHEW!
IT'S ... NOT ... TRUE ...
... WHAT I DO ... I DO TO ... HELP JUDAH!
AND WHAT I DO, I DO TO HELP JUDAH AS WELL.
UHNF!

LEAVE HIM ALONE!
YOU'RE KILLING HIM!
STAY BACK, OR WE'LL BE KILLING YOU AS WELL ...

AHHHNN!

TAKE HIM AWAY.
LOCK HIM UP.
WHAT ARE YOU DOING?
WHERE ARE YOU TAKING HIM?
LET ME GO!
IF I WERE YOU, I WOULD NOT BE SEEN WITH THE LIKES OF HIM.
IF YOU TRULY WISH TO SERVE YOUR COUNTRY, YOU SHOULD NOT SERVE HIM.
JEREMIAH IS A MAN OF GOD, AND --
ENOUGH, BARUCH.
CAPTAIN IRIJAH.
TELL ME WHERE YOU ARE TAKING JEREMIAH.
OR I WILL USE WHAT LITTLE POLITICAL POWER I HAVE LEFT TO DESTROY YOU AND YOUR CAREER FOREVER.
...

The house of Jonathan the secretary, recently converted to a prison.
THIS IS JONATHAN THE SECRETARY'S HOUSE.
NOT ANY LONGER.
WHAT HAS THIS CITY COME TO?

BARUCH, IT IS LATE.
THERE IS NOTHING MORE YOU CAN DO TONIGHT.
GO HOME. GET SOME REST.

NO. I WILL STAY HERE.

VERY WELL.

SLAP!
AAHK!
HUHN?
SLAP!
OOFFF ...
THUD!
UHN!
SLAP!
UHN!
THUD!
OOOOH ...

HMMMM ...

ALL NIGHT, IDDO ...
ALL NIGHT.

BARUCH, THERE IS NOTHING WE CAN DO HERE.
LET'S GO AND SEE IF WE CAN FIND SOMEONE WHO CAN HELP US.

WHO?
THE ONLY LEADERS LEFT HERE SUPPORT ZEDEKIAH!
PERHAPS WE GO TO ZEDEKIAH!
YOU THINK HE'S GOING TO HELP US?

NO.
SO LET'S THINK OF SOME BETTER IDEAS --
IDDO?

NOW WHAT?
I DON'T KNOW.

THE PALACE?
WHAT? ZEDEKIAH WANTS TO SEE HIM GET BEATEN PERSONALLY NOW?
I DON'T KNOW ...

WHAT IS GOING ON?
SHUT UP!

STAY HERE.
I --

STAY!

SLAM!

JEREMIAH?

MY KING ...
STOP WITH THE FALSE HONORIFICS!
NO, YOU ARE MY KING.

JEREMIAH, I BROUGHT YOU HERE FOR A REASON.
THE BABYLONIANS HAVE RETREATED.
I WANT TO KNOW ...

IS THERE ANY WORD FROM THE LORD?

YES.

YOU WILL BE HANDED OVER TO THE KING OF BABYLON.
NO!!!
THAT IS NOT WHAT YOU WERE TO SAY!
WHAT DO YOU WANT?
THOSE OTHER PROPHETS BRING YOU THE WORDS YOU WANT.
I BRING YOU THE LORD'S WORDS.
WAIT!

PLEASE, TELL ME, WHAT CRIME HAVE I COMMITTED?
WHAT HAVE I DONE WRONG TO YOU OR YOUR OFFICIALS?
WHERE ARE THE OTHER PROPHETS?

WHERE ARE THE PROPHETS WHO TOLD YOU THAT BABYLON WOULD ***NOT*** ATTACK YOU?
AND YET I, WHOSE WORDS WERE REVEALED TO BE TRUTH, AM BEATEN AND IMPRISONED!

PLEASE. I HAVE ONE REQUEST.
PLEASE, DO NOT SEND ME BACK TO THAT PRISON.
I WILL DIE THERE.

The courtyard of the guard.

WHY ARE YOU BRINGING HIM HERE?
BY ORDER OF THE KING.
WE HAVE THE INSTRUCTIONS HERE, WITH HIS SEAL.

ALL RIGHT.
THERE'S A CELL ON THE WESTERN CORNER. TAKE HIM THERE.

BLASTED BUREAUCRACIES!

Jeremiah remained in the courtyard of the guard for a season.
BARUCH, PLEASE HIRE SOME SCRIBES TO ALLOW COPIES OF MY MESSAGE TO BE SPREAD THROUGHOUT JERUSALEM.
JEREMIAH, I DON'T THINK PEOPLE ARE GOING TO PARTICULARLY LIKE YOUR MESSAGE!
THIS IS WHY THEY CALL YOU A TRAITOR!
THIS IS WHY I AM A PATRIOT!
I WILL NOT SACRIFICE THE TRUTH FOR CONVENIENCE!
BUT JEREMIAH!
"WHOEVER STAYS IN THE CITY WILL DIE BY SWORD, FAMINE OR PLAGUE, BUT WHOEVER GOES OVER TO THE BABYLONIANS WILL LIVE!"
DO NOT THINK THAT JUST BECAUSE YOU ARE IN PRISON YOU ARE UNTOUCHABLE!
IDDO, YOU KNOW I KNOW THE RISKS.
AND IF YOU WERE IN MY POSITION, YOU KNOW YOU WOULD DO THE SAME THING!
YES.
I WOULD.
EVERYTHING WILL BE FINE.

The throne room of Zedekiah.
HE SHOULD BE PUT TO DEATH!
HE IS DISCOURAGING THE SOLDIERS WHO ARE LEFT IN THE CITY AND ALL THE PEOPLE!
HE SAID, "THIS CITY WILL CERTAINLY BE HANDED OVER TO THE ARMY OF THE KING OF BABYLON!"
THIS MAN SEEKS NOT THE GOOD OF THE PEOPLE, BUT HE REJOICES IN THE POSSIBILITY OF OUR RUIN!
HMMM.
HE IS IN YOUR HANDS.
THE KING CAN DO NOTHING TO OPPOSE YOU.
The courtyard of the guard.
WE'VE COME FOR JEREMIAH.
IS HE BEING RELOCATED AGAIN?
NOT EXACTLY.
WHERE ARE YOU TAKING ME?

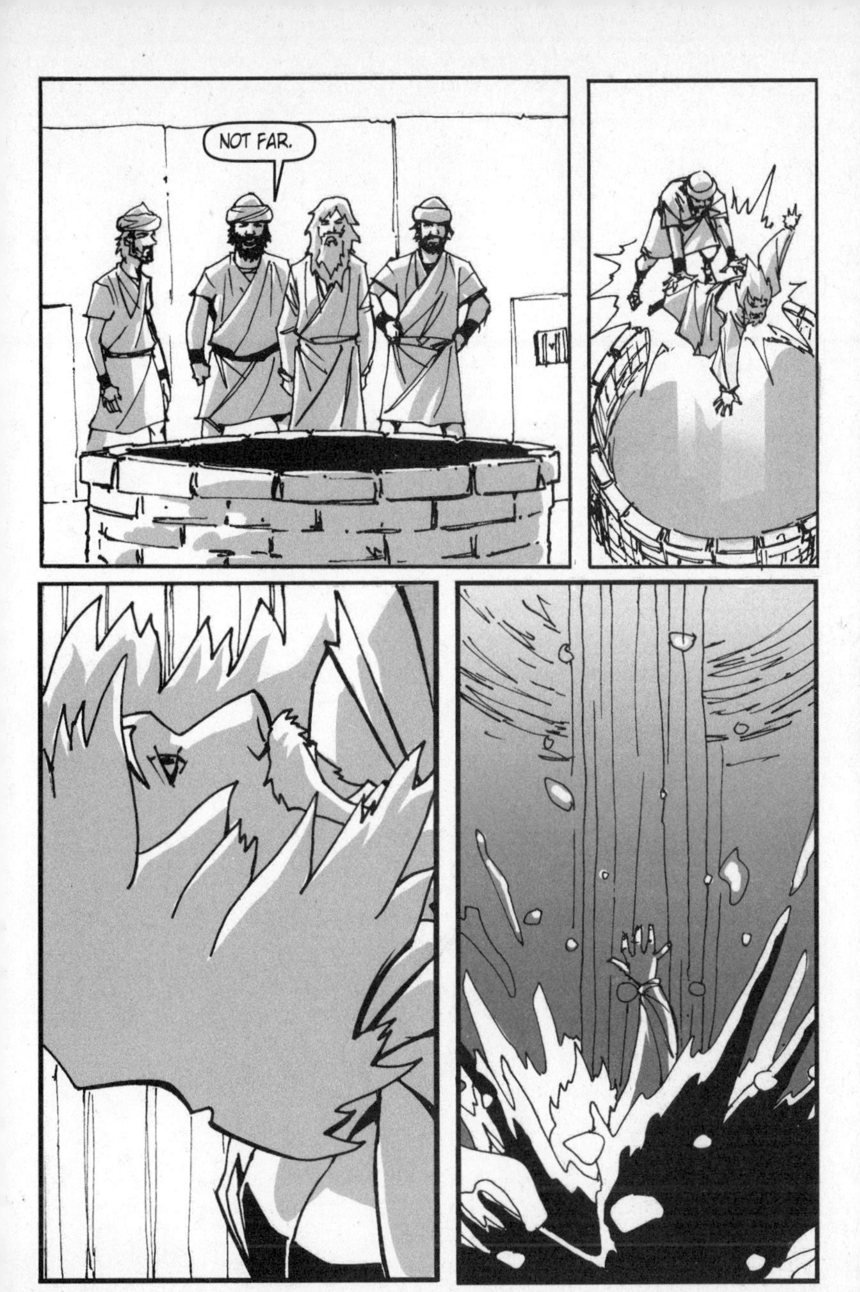
NOT FAR.

BWA-HA-HAW!!!

OUR ORDERS ARE TO LET YOU STARVE!
THEY ARE ORDERS WE WILL GLADLY FOLLOW!
AH-HAHAHAW!!!

BWA-HA-HAW!!!

"I am the man who has seen affliction by the rod of his wrath.
"He has driven me away and made me walk in darkness rather than light.

"Indeed, he has turned his hand against me again and again, all day long.
"He has made my skin and flesh grow old and has broken my bones.

"He has besieged me and surrounded me with bitterness and hardship.

"He has made me dwell in darkness like those long dead.
"He has walled me in so I cannot escape."

The Benjamin Gate of Jerusalem.
THE KING IS HOLDING COURT AT THE BENJAMIN GATE TODAY ...
AND YOU PLAN TO TALK TO THE KING?
IF I CAN GET AUDIENCE!
I MAY HAVE A BETTER IDEA THAN JUST MARCHING INTO THE COURT OF THE KING ...
WHAT?
I KNOW SOMEONE ... SOMEONE MORE LIKELY TO LISTEN TO OUR CASE ... AND MORE LIKELY TO BE LISTENED *TO* BY THE KING ...

EBED-MELECH! HELLO, MY OLD FRIEND!
IDDO! IT'S BEEN TOO LONG.
TO WHAT DO I OWE THE PLEASURE OF YOUR VISIT?
THE PROPHET JEREMIAH ...
NOW, IDDO, I CANNOT HELP YOU THERE.
THE KING WILL NOT GO AGAINST HIS ADVISORS IN THAT REGARD.
MY FRIEND, THEY HAVE TOSSED HIM INTO AN EMPTY CISTERN, WHERE THEY INTEND TO LET HIM STARVE!
THIS MAN IS A PROPHET OF GOD. HE HAS DONE NO WRONG.
I ... I CAN'T JUST ...
... I'LL SEE WHAT I CAN DO.

JEREMIAH!

WHO ... WHO'S THERE?

IT'S ME, JEREMIAH! BARUCH!

THEY ... THEY THREW ME IN A WELL.

YES, JEREMIAH.
I KNOW. BUT IT'S ALL OVER NOW.

THE KING HAS ORDERED YOUR RELEASE FROM THE WELL.
I'M AFRAID YOU HAVE TO STAY IN THE PRISON, THOUGH.

ARE YOU OKAY?
IS THERE ANYTHING YOU NEED?

I'M HUNGRY. THIRSTY.
AND I NEED A BATH.

ALL THREE ARE THINGS I CAN PROVIDE EASILY.

WHEN WILL THEY LEARN ...
... THEY CAN SILENCE ME, BUT THEY CANNOT SILENCE GOD.

CHAPTER FIVE

"Fuel for the Flames"

... THIS IS WHAT THE LORD ALMIGHTY, THE GOD OF ISRAEL, SAYS: "WHEN I BRING THEM BACK FROM CAPTIVITY, THE PEOPLE IN THE LAND OF JUDAH WILL ONCE AGAIN USE THESE WORDS:

"'THE LORD BLESS YOU, O RIGHTEOUS DWELLING, O SACRED MOUNTAIN.'
"PEOPLE WILL LIVE TOGETHER IN JUDAH AND ALL ITS TOWNS -- FARMERS AND THOSE WHO MOVE ABOUT WITH THEIR FLOCKS.
"I WILL REFRESH THE WEARY AND SATISFY THE FAINT."

IS THAT ALL?
THAT'S ALL THE LORD SAID IN MY DREAM.
IT WAS A PLEASANT SLEEP, TO BE SURE.
WOULD YOU SAY IT REFRESHED AND SATISFIED YOU, JEREMIAH?

YOU COULD SAY THAT --
HNM?

JEREMIAH.
IT SEEMS THAT YOU ARE TO ACCOMPANY THESE GENTLEMEN.

WHERE ARE YOU TAKING ME?

WE ARE NOT AT LIBERTY TO SAY, SIR.

THEN TELL ME WHERE YOU ARE **NOT** TAKING ME.
ARE YOU TAKING ME TO THE HOUSE OF JONATHAN THE SECRETARY?

ANSWER HIM.

NO, SIR.

THEN I WILL GO WITH YOU.

BARUCH, TELL IDDO TO MEET US HERE TONIGHT.
I WISH TO SPEAK WITH HIM.
AND SHOW HIM THESE NEW WORDS.

VERY WELL.
LET US GO.

THIS IS WHERE YOU ARE TAKING ME?

COME.

THANK YOU, JEREMIAH, FOR COMING TO MEET ME.

MY KING. TO WHAT DO I OWE THIS PLEASURE?

I HAVE A QUESTION.
DO NOT HIDE ANYTHING FROM ME. JUST ANSWER MY QUESTION.

BHAH!
EVEN IF I GAVE YOU MY ANSWER, YOU WOULD NOT LISTEN!
OR YOU'D KILL ME!

OR BOTH.

NO.
I WILL LISTEN.

SIGH.
YOUR FAMILY HAS NOT LISTENED TO ME SINCE YOUR FATHER JOSIAH WAS ON THE THRONE.

AND THAT WAS BECAUSE THE MESSAGES THE LORD GAVE TO ME WHILE YOUR FATHER WAS ON THE THRONE WERE MOSTLY ABOUT YOU!

PLEASE!
YOU HAVE MY WORD; I WILL NOT KILL YOU!
NOR WILL I TURN YOU OVER TO THOSE WHO WANT YOU DEAD!
AS SURELY AS THE LORD WHO GIVES US BREATH LIVES ...

YOU GIVE ME YOUR WORD THAT YOU WILL NOT KILL ME.
I MAY BELIEVE THAT.
BUT DO YOU GIVE ME YOUR WORD THAT YOU WILL HEED MY MESSAGE?

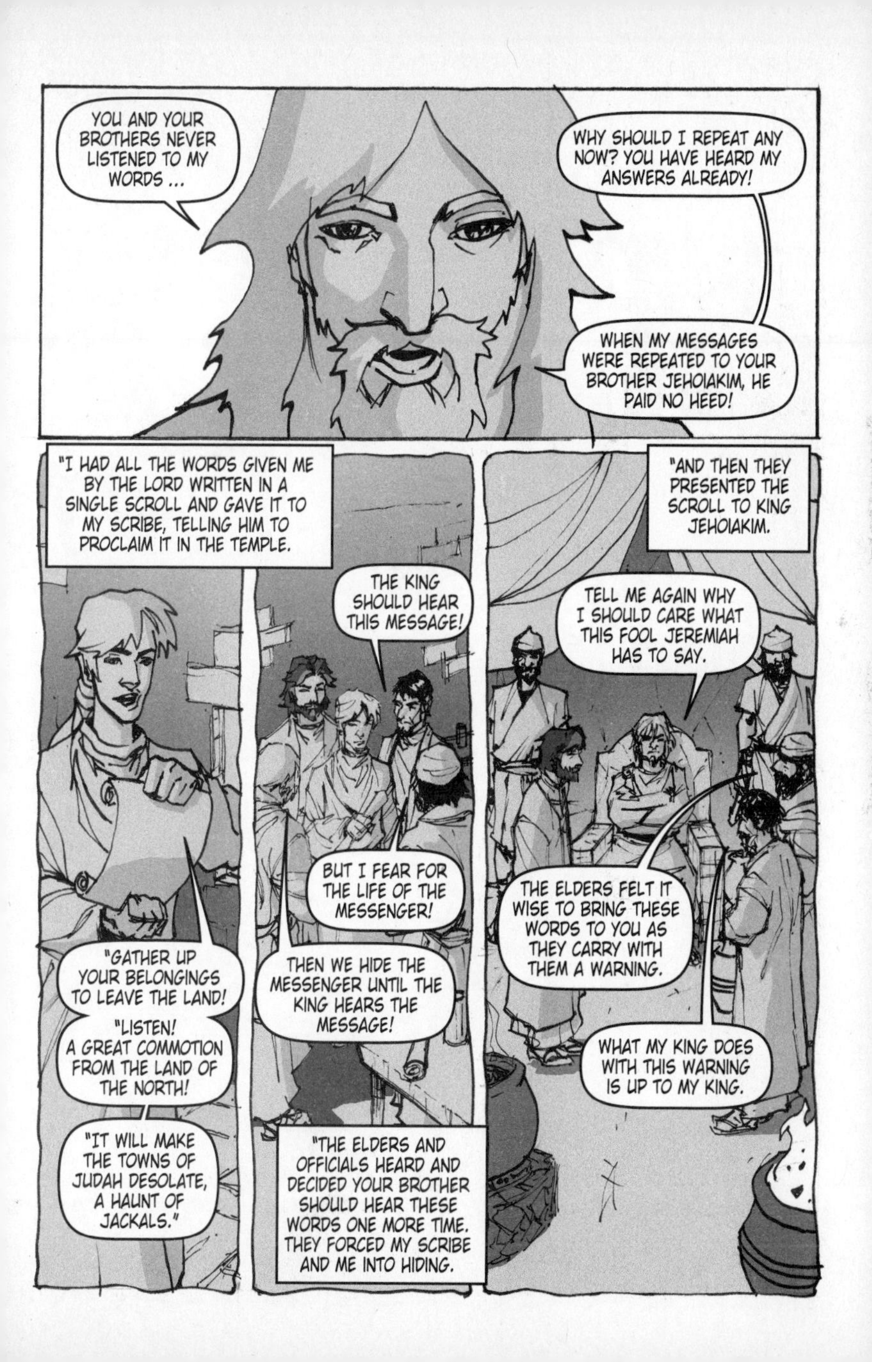
YOU AND YOUR BROTHERS NEVER LISTENED TO MY WORDS ...
WHY SHOULD I REPEAT ANY NOW? YOU HAVE HEARD MY ANSWERS ALREADY!
WHEN MY MESSAGES WERE REPEATED TO YOUR BROTHER JEHOIAKIM, HE PAID NO HEED!
"I HAD ALL THE WORDS GIVEN ME BY THE LORD WRITTEN IN A SINGLE SCROLL AND GAVE IT TO MY SCRIBE, TELLING HIM TO PROCLAIM IT IN THE TEMPLE.
"GATHER UP YOUR BELONGINGS TO LEAVE THE LAND!
"LISTEN! A GREAT COMMOTION FROM THE LAND OF THE NORTH!
"IT WILL MAKE THE TOWNS OF JUDAH DESOLATE, A HAUNT OF JACKALS."
THE KING SHOULD HEAR THIS MESSAGE!
BUT I FEAR FOR THE LIFE OF THE MESSENGER!
THEN WE HIDE THE MESSENGER UNTIL THE KING HEARS THE MESSAGE!
"THE ELDERS AND OFFICIALS HEARD AND DECIDED YOUR BROTHER SHOULD HEAR THESE WORDS ONE MORE TIME. THEY FORCED MY SCRIBE AND ME INTO HIDING.
"AND THEN THEY PRESENTED THE SCROLL TO KING JEHOIAKIM.
TELL ME AGAIN WHY I SHOULD CARE WHAT THIS FOOL JEREMIAH HAS TO SAY.
THE ELDERS FELT IT WISE TO BRING THESE WORDS TO YOU AS THEY CARRY WITH THEM A WARNING.
WHAT MY KING DOES WITH THIS WARNING IS UP TO MY KING.

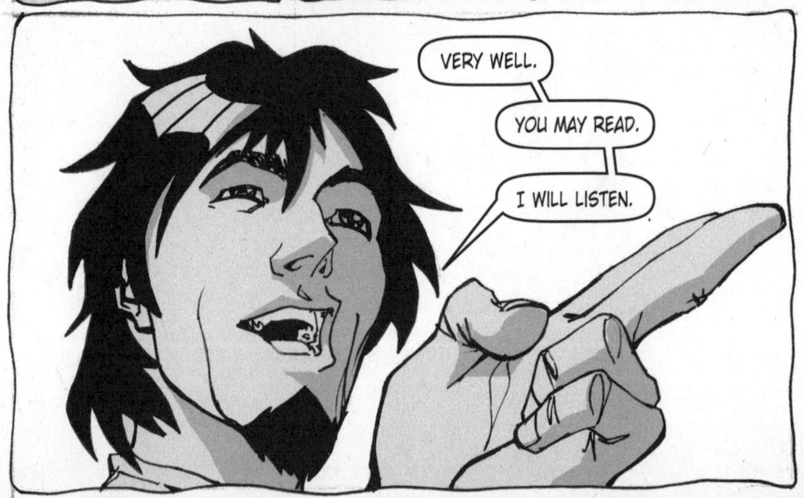
VERY WELL.
YOU MAY READ.
I WILL LISTEN.

...

...

ON WITH IT, MAN!

YES.
SIR.
AHEM!
"'I REMEMBER THE DEVOTION OF YOUR YOUTH, HOW AS A BRIDE YOU LOVED ME AND FOLLOWED ME THROUGH THE DESERT.

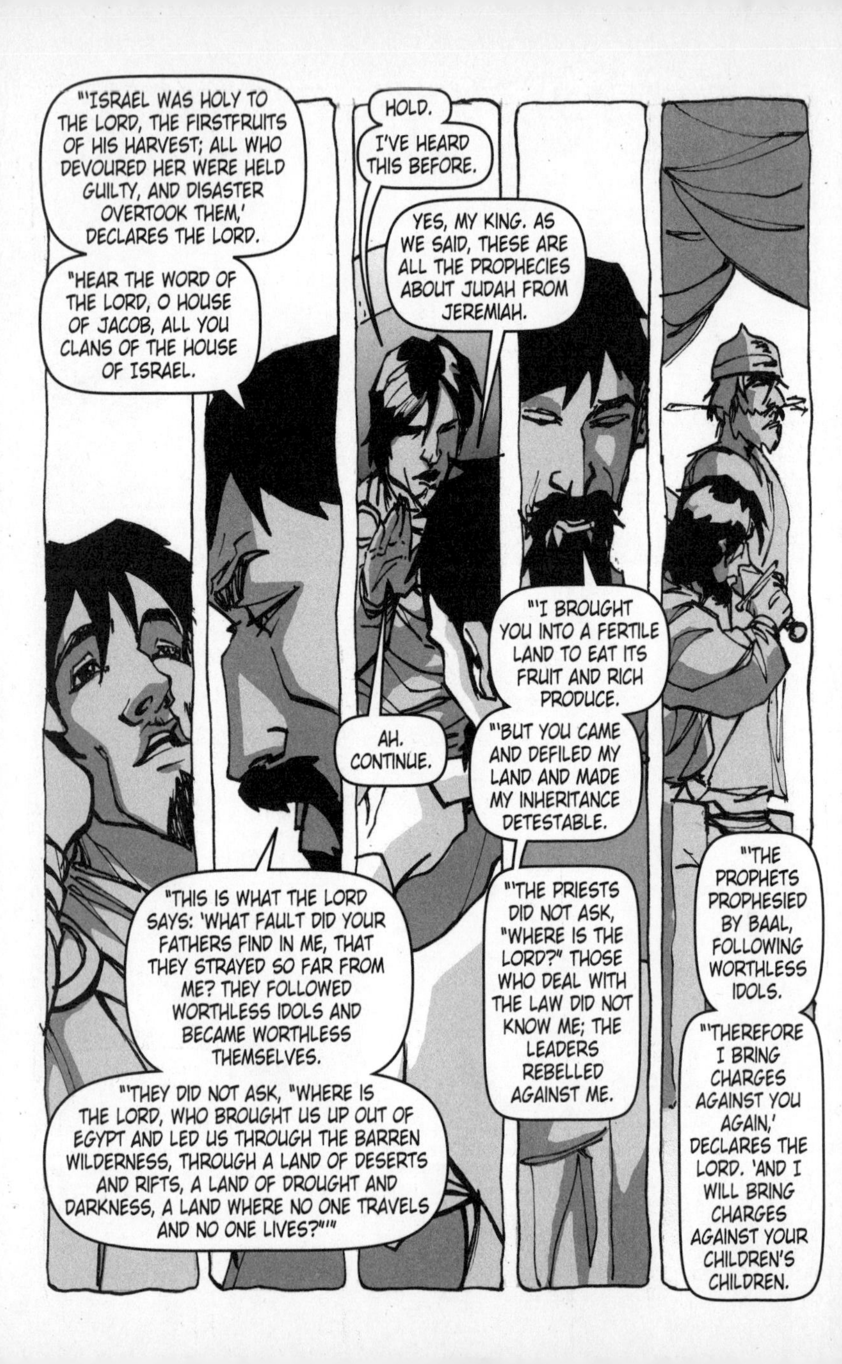
"'ISRAEL WAS HOLY TO THE LORD, THE FIRSTFRUITS OF HIS HARVEST; ALL WHO DEVOURED HER WERE HELD GUILTY, AND DISASTER OVERTOOK THEM,' DECLARES THE LORD.
"HEAR THE WORD OF THE LORD, O HOUSE OF JACOB, ALL YOU CLANS OF THE HOUSE OF ISRAEL.
"THIS IS WHAT THE LORD SAYS: 'WHAT FAULT DID YOUR FATHERS FIND IN ME, THAT THEY STRAYED SO FAR FROM ME? THEY FOLLOWED WORTHLESS IDOLS AND BECAME WORTHLESS THEMSELVES.
"'THEY DID NOT ASK, "WHERE IS THE LORD, WHO BROUGHT US UP OUT OF EGYPT AND LED US THROUGH THE BARREN WILDERNESS, THROUGH A LAND OF DESERTS AND RIFTS, A LAND OF DROUGHT AND DARKNESS, A LAND WHERE NO ONE TRAVELS AND NO ONE LIVES?"'"
HOLD.
I'VE HEARD THIS BEFORE.
YES, MY KING. AS WE SAID, THESE ARE ALL THE PROPHECIES ABOUT JUDAH FROM JEREMIAH.
AH. CONTINUE.
"'I BROUGHT YOU INTO A FERTILE LAND TO EAT ITS FRUIT AND RICH PRODUCE.
"'BUT YOU CAME AND DEFILED MY LAND AND MADE MY INHERITANCE DETESTABLE.
"'THE PRIESTS DID NOT ASK, "WHERE IS THE LORD?" THOSE WHO DEAL WITH THE LAW DID NOT KNOW ME; THE LEADERS REBELLED AGAINST ME.
"'THE PROPHETS PROPHESIED BY BAAL, FOLLOWING WORTHLESS IDOLS.
"'THEREFORE I BRING CHARGES AGAINST YOU AGAIN,' DECLARES THE LORD. 'AND I WILL BRING CHARGES AGAINST YOUR CHILDREN'S CHILDREN.

"'CROSS OVER TO THE COASTS OF KITTIM AND LOOK, SEND TO KEDAR AND SERVE CLOSELY; SEE IF THERE HAS EVER BEEN ANYTHING LIKE THIS:
"'HAS A NATION EVER CHANGED ITS GODS? (YET THEY ARE NOT GODS AT ALL.) BUT MY PEOPLE HAVE EXCHANGED THEIR GLORY FOR WORTHLESS IDOLS.
"'BE APPALLED AT THIS, O HEAVENS, AND SHUDDER WITH GREAT HORROR,' DECLARES THE LORD.
"'MY PEOPLE HAVE COMMITTED TWO SINS: THEY HAVE FORSAKEN ME, THE SPRING OF LIVING WATER, AND HAVE DUG THEIR OWN CISTERNS, BROKEN CISTERNS THAT CANNOT HOLD WATER.
"'IS ISRAEL A SERVANT, A SLAVE BY BIRTH? WHY THEN HAS HE BECOME PLUNDER? LIONS HAVE ROARED; THEY HAVE GROWLED AT HIM.'"

AH ...
"'THEY HAVE LAID WASTE HIS LAND; HIS TOWNS ARE BURNED AND DESERTED.
"'ALSO, THE MEN OF MEMPHIS AND TAHPANHES HAVE SHAVED THE CROWN OF YOUR HEAD.
"'HAVE YOU NOT BROUGHT THIS ON YOURSELVES BY FORSAKING THE LORD YOUR GOD WHEN HE LED YOU IN THE WAY?
"'NOW WHY GO TO EGYPT TO DRINK WATER FROM THE SHIHOR? AND WHY GO TO ASSYRIA TO DRINK WATER FROM THE RIVER?
"'YOUR WICKEDNESS WILL PUNISH YOU; YOUR BACKSLIDING WILL REBUKE YOU.
"'CONSIDER THEN AND REALIZE HOW EVIL AND BITTER IT IS FOR YOU WHEN YOU FORSAKE THE LORD YOUR GOD AND HAVE NO AWE OF ME,' DECLARES THE LORD, THE LORD ALMIGHTY.

"'LONG AGO YOU BROKE OFF YOUR YOKE AND TORE OFF YOUR BONDS; YOU SAID, "I WILL NOT SERVE YOU!"'"
UH ...
"'INDEED, ON EVERY HIGH HILL AND UNDER EVERY SPREADING TREE YOU LAY DOWN AS A PROSTITUTE.
"'I HAD PLANTED YOU LIKE A CHOICE VINE OF SOUND AND RELIABLE STOCK. HOW THEN DID YOU TURN AGAINST ME INTO A CORRUPT, WILD VINE?
"'ALTHOUGH YOU WASH YOURSELF WITH SODA AND USE AN ABUNDANCE OF SOAP, THE STAIN OF YOUR GUILT IS STILL BEFORE ME,' DECLARES THE SOVEREIGN LORD.
"'HOW CAN YOU SAY, "I AM NOT DEFILED; I HAVE NOT RUN AFTER THE BAALS"? SEE HOW YOU BEHAVED IN THE VALLEY; CONSIDER WHAT YOU HAVE DONE.
"'THEY SAY TO WOOD, "YOU ARE MY FATHER," AND TO STONE, "YOU GAVE ME BIRTH." THEY HAVE TURNED THEIR BACKS TO ME AND NOT THEIR FACES; YET WHEN THEY ARE IN TROUBLE, THEY SAY, "COME AND SAVE US!"'"
HE --
WAIT!

...
PLEASE, CONTINUE.
"'WHERE THEN ARE THE GODS YOU MADE FOR YOURSELVES?
"'LET THEM COME IF THEY CAN SAVE YOU WHEN YOU ARE IN TROUBLE!
"'FOR YOU HAVE AS MANY GODS AS YOU HAVE TOWNS, O JUDAH.
"'WHY DO YOU BRING CHARGES AGAINST ME? YOU HAVE ALL REBELLED AGAINST ME,' DECLARES THE LORD.
"'IN VAIN I PUNISHED YOUR PEOPLE; THEY DID NOT RESPOND TO CORRECTION.
"'YOUR SWORD HAS DEVOURED YOUR PROPHETS LIKE A RAVENING LION.

"'YOU OF THIS GENERATION, CONSIDER THE WORD OF THE LORD:
"'HAVE I BEEN A DESERT TO ISRAEL OR A LAND OF GREAT DARKNESS?
"'WHY DO MY PEOPLE SAY, "WE ARE FREE TO ROAM; WE WILL COME TO YOU NO MORE"?
"'DOES A MAIDEN FORGET HER JEWELRY, A BRIDE HER WEDDING ORNAMENTS?
"YET MY PEOPLE HAVE FORGOTTEN ME, DAYS WITHOUT NUMBER.
"YET IN SPITE OF ALL THIS YOU SAY, "I AM INNOCENT; HE IS NOT ANGRY WITH ME." BUT I WILL PASS JUDGMENT ON YOU BECAUSE YOU SAY, "I HAVE NOT SINNED."
"'WHY DO YOU GO ABOUT SO MUCH, CHANGING YOUR WAYS? YOU WILL BE DISAPPOINTED BY EGYPT AS YOU WERE BY ASSYRIA.
"'YOU WILL ALSO LEAVE THAT PLACE WITH YOUR HANDS ON YOUR HEAD, FOR THE LORD HAS REJECTED THOSE YOU TRUST; YOU WILL NOT BE HELPED BY THEM.'"
MY KING! THOSE WORDS SIMPLY CANNOT BE BURNED!
THEY CAN'T?
HMM, NO, IT SEEMS THAT THEY BURN QUITE WELL ...
AH, HERE IT SEEMS TO BE JEREMIAH SPEAKING ... "YOU ARE ALWAYS RIGHTEOUS, O LORD, WHEN I BRING A CASE BEFORE YOU. YET I WOULD SPEAK WITH YOU ABOUT YOUR JUSTICE: WHY DOES THE WAY OF THE WICKED PROSPER?

"WHY DO ALL THE FAITHLESS LIVE AT EASE?
"YOU HAVE PLANTED THEM, AND THEY HAVE TAKEN ROOT; THEY GROW AND BEAR FRUIT.
"YOU ARE ALWAYS ON THEIR LIPS BUT FAR FROM THEIR HEARTS."
AND HERE IS THE LORD'S ANSWER: "'I WILL FORSAKE MY HOUSE, ABANDON MY INHERITANCE; I WILL GIVE THE ONE I LOVE INTO THE HANDS OF HER ENEMIES.
"'OVER ALL THE BARREN HEIGHTS IN THE DESERT DESTROYERS WILL SWARM, FOR THE SWORD OF THE LORD WILL DEVOUR FROM ONE END OF THE LAND TO THE OTHER; NO ONE WILL BE SAFE.
"'A SCORCHING WIND FROM THE BARREN HEIGHTS IN THE DESERT BLOWS TOWARD MY PEOPLE, BUT NOT TO WINNOW OR CLEANSE.'"

"WHEN THE ELDERS CAME TO REPORT WHAT YOUR BROTHER HAD DONE, MY SCRIBE AND I WERE WAITING.
IDDO, JEREMIAH HAS A RESPONSE FOR KING JEHOIAKIM.
ALREADY? WE HAVEN'T EVEN TOLD YOU --
JEREMIAH HAS A FASTER SOURCE OF INFORMATION.
HERE.
WHAT'S THIS?
THE LORD TOLD JEREMIAH TO WRITE IT OUT AGAIN ...

IS IT ME, OR IS THIS SCROLL LONGER?
YES, ABOUT THAT, JEREMIAH WAS TOLD TO ADD SOME NEW WORDS ...

"THE NEW WORDS WERE SPECIFICALLY ADDED FOR JEHOIAKIM.

"'HE WILL HAVE NO ONE TO SIT ON THE THRONE OF DAVID; HIS BODY WILL BE THROWN OUT AND EXPOSED TO THE HEAT BY DAY AND THE FROST BY NIGHT.
"'I WILL PUNISH HIM AND HIS CHILDREN AND HIS ATTENDANTS FOR THEIR WICKEDNESS; I WILL BRING ON THEM AND THOSE LIVING IN JERUSALEM AND THE PEOPLE OF JUDAH EVERY DISASTER I PRONOUNCED AGAINST THEM, BECAUSE THEY HAVE NOT LISTENED.'"

YOU SWEAR BY THE GOD WHO GIVES US BREATH THAT YOU WILL NOT KILL ME.
BUT YOU ASK ME TO WASTE GOD-GIVEN BREATH REPEATING WHAT YOU ALREADY KNOW?
PLEASE.

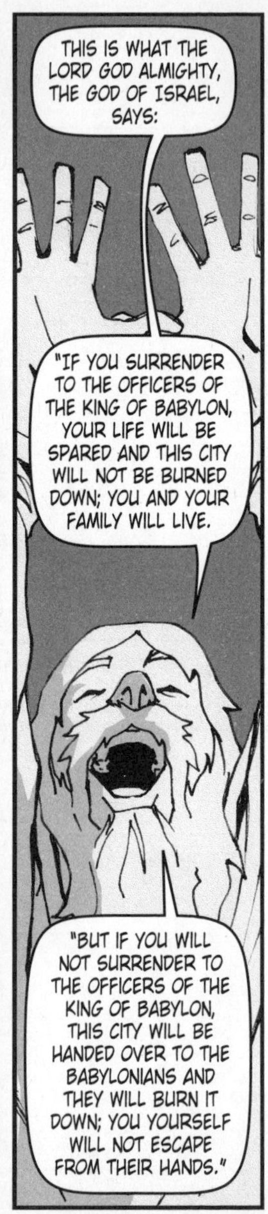
THIS IS WHAT THE LORD GOD ALMIGHTY, THE GOD OF ISRAEL, SAYS:
"IF YOU SURRENDER TO THE OFFICERS OF THE KING OF BABYLON, YOUR LIFE WILL BE SPARED AND THIS CITY WILL NOT BE BURNED DOWN; YOU AND YOUR FAMILY WILL LIVE.
"BUT IF YOU WILL NOT SURRENDER TO THE OFFICERS OF THE KING OF BABYLON, THIS CITY WILL BE HANDED OVER TO THE BABYLONIANS AND THEY WILL BURN IT DOWN; YOU YOURSELF WILL NOT ESCAPE FROM THEIR HANDS."

...

IF I DO THAT -- SURRENDER, AS YOU'VE BEEN TELLING ME TO -- WHAT WILL HAPPEN TO ME?
WHAT OF THE JEWS IN BABYLON? IF I AM TAKEN TO BABYLON, THEY WILL WANT ME TO PAY FOR SURRENDERING.

JUST OBEY THE LORD.
YOUR LIFE WILL BE SPARED.
BUT IF YOU DO NOT OBEY ...

... ALL YOUR WIVES AND CHILDREN WILL BE BROUGHT OUT TO THE BABYLONIANS.
YOU CANNOT ESCAPE; YOU WILL BE CAPTURED.
AND THIS CITY WILL BE BURNED TO THE GROUND.
BURNED LIKE THE PIECES OF SCROLL THAT YOUR BROTHER TOSSED SO CARELESSLY INTO THE FIREPOT ...

T-WHEET!!!

DO NOT TELL ANYONE
OF THIS MEETING,
JEREMIAH.

... THE WHOLE VALLEY WHERE DEAD BODIES AND ASHES ARE THROWN, AND ALL THE TERRACES OUT TO THE KIDRON VALLEY ON THE EAST AS FAR AS THE CORNER OF THE HORSE GATE, WILL BE HOLY TO THE LORD.
THE CITY WILL NEVER AGAIN BE UPROOTED OR DEMOLISHED.

BARUCH, IT'S A LITTLE LATE FOR YOU TO BE WORKING, IS IT NOT?
IT'S ONLY LATE FOR OLD MEN LIKE US, IDDO.

HELLO, SIRS.
HE IS HERE AT MY REQUEST.
I HAD TO GET SOME THINGS WRITTEN OUT QUICKLY.

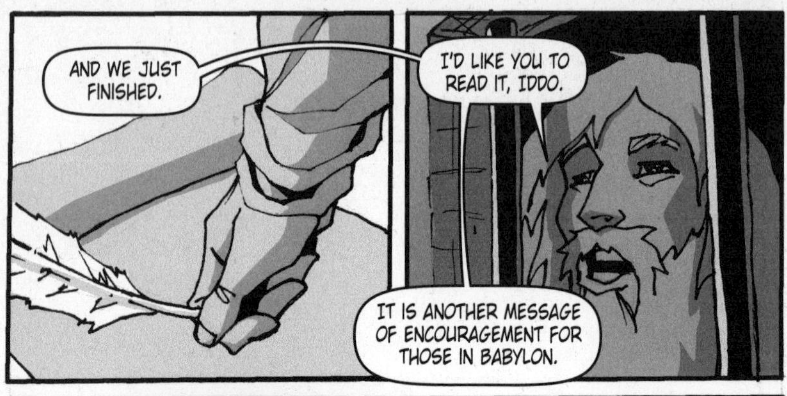
AND WE JUST FINISHED.
I'D LIKE YOU TO READ IT, IDDO.
IT IS ANOTHER MESSAGE OF ENCOURAGEMENT FOR THOSE IN BABYLON.

I WOULD LIKE TO SEE SOME COPIES MADE.
AND THEN, PERHAPS, HAVE SOME PEOPLE DISTRIBUTE IT TO THE EXILES.

THERE ARE SOME GREAT PROMISES HERE, BUT EACH PROMISE SEEMS TO BE CONTINGENT ON GREAT TRAGEDY.
SOMETIMES THAT IS THE WAY OF THINGS.

SOMETIMES, THE PROPHECIES OF THE LORD ARE EITHER/OR PROPOSITIONS.
EITHER DO THIS, OR DO THAT.
AND EACH CHOICE CARRIES ITS OWN OUTCOME.

YES.
AND YOU HAVE GIVEN SUCH A MESSAGE TO ZEDEKIAH.
I HAVE.

AND YOU BELIEVE ZEDEKIAH'S CHOICE IS CLEAR?

YES.
JERUSALEM WILL BURN.

BUT OUT OF THE ASHES WILL COME BEAUTY.
AND IT IS THAT WHICH THOSE IN BABYLON SHOULD KNOW.
SHOULD LOOK FORWARD TO.
SO THIS MESSAGE SHOULD BE TAKEN TO THEM.
SO THAT WHEN NEWS OF JERUSALEM'S DESTRUCTION REACHES THEIR EARS, THEY WILL HAVE ALREADY HEARD NEWS OF JERUSALEM'S REBIRTH.
I WILL TAKE IT.
I WILL TAKE YOUR MESSAGE TO THEM.
IDDO, ARE YOU SURE?
YOUR AGE --
MEANS NOTHING.
I HAVE STAYED AND DONE ALL I COULD FOR OUR NATION.
IT IS GOING TO BURN REGARDLESS.

I CAN SERVE MY PEOPLE BETTER IF I AM WITH THEM NOW.
WE HAVE SERVED OUR NATION BY SERVING IN THE TEMPLE, BY SERVING JEREMIAH, BY SERVING THE OFFICIALS.
BUT SOON THERE WILL BE NO TEMPLE. AND IF JEREMIAH'S WORDS ARE TRUE -- AND HAVE THEY EVER BEEN UNTRUE? -- SOON THERE WILL BE NO OFFICIALS.

NO.
I WILL TAKE THIS MESSAGE OF HOPE TO THE EXILES.
TO OUR NATION.
TO MY FAMILY.

I LEAVE THIS CITY TO THE YOUNGER GENERATION!

ARE YOU SURE ABOUT THIS?

And Jeremiah remained in the courtyard of the guard until the day Jerusalem was captured.

CHAPTER SIX

"The Fall of Jerusalem"

This is how Jerusalem was taken:
In the ninth year of Zedekiah king of Judah, Nebuchadnezzar king of Babylon marched against Jerusalem with his whole army and laid siege to it.
And on the ninth day of the fourth month of Zedekiah's eleventh year, the city wall was broken through.

I SHOULD HAVE SURRENDERED ...
TOO LATE FOR THAT NOW!
When Zedekiah king of Judah and all the soldiers saw the Babylonians enter the gate, they fled.
THEIR FORCES WILL COME THROUGH THE BREACHES IN OUR WALL ON THE OTHER SIDE OF THE CITY!
They left the city at night by way of the king's garden …
… through the gate between the two walls …
… and headed toward the Arabah.

But the Babylonian army pursued them.
And overtook Zedekiah in the plains of Jericho.
They captured him and took him to Nebuchadnezzar king of Babylon at Riblah in the land of Hamath.
There at Riblah the king of Babylon pronounced sentence on him.
YOU WERE A FOOL TO STAND AGAINST ME!
BABYLON IS ETERNAL! YOUR INSIGNIFICANT LITTLE TRIBE IS NOTHING!
WHAT ARE YOU DOING?

WHAT IS HAPPENING?
PLEASE ... HELP ...
WHY?!?
NO ... PLEASE DON'T ...
NO ...
There at Riblah the king of Babylon killed all the nobles of Judah.
BRING IN THE ROYAL SPAWN OF THIS MUD GUPPY!
WHAT ... WAIT ... WHAT ARE YOU DOING NOW?

WHAT ARE YOU DOING?
FATHER?
WHAT IS HAPPENING?
FATHER, HELP ...
NOOOOOOOOOOOO!!!!!!!
There at Riblah the king of Babylon slaughtered the sons of Zedekiah before his eyes.
NOW, TO MAKE SURE THAT IS THE LAST THING YOU SEE.

IS THAT TO BE THE LAST THING I SEE BEFORE I DIE?
NOT EXACTLY.
NOOO!!!
AHHHHHHH!!!
Then he put out Zedekiah's eyes and bound him with bronze shackles to take him to Babylon.

The Babylonians set fire to the royal palace and the houses of the people and broke down the walls of Jerusalem.
Nebuzaradan, commander of the imperial guard, carried into exile to Babylon the people who remained in the city, along with those who had gone over to him, and the rest of the people.
But Nebuzaradan, the commander of the guard, left behind in the land of Judah some of the poor people, who owned nothing; and at that time he gave them vineyards and fields.
Now Nebuchadnezzar, king of Babylon, had given these orders about Jeremiah through Nebuzaradan, commander of the imperial guard: "Take him and look after him; don't harm him but do for him whatever he asks."

THIS IS AS GOOD A PLACE AS ANY TO KEEP OUR PRISONERS ...
WHO ARE YOU, PRISONER?
I AM JEREMIAH OF ANATHOTH, SON OF HILKIAH.
AHH. SO YOU'RE THE ONE WE WERE TOLD OF.
YOU ARE TO LET THIS ONE GO, WITHOUT HARMING HIM!
WE HAVE PLACED GEDALIAH IN CHARGE, JEREMIAH.
HE WILL BE THE NEW REGIONAL GOVERNOR.
MY KING HAS SEEN TO IT THAT YOUR LINE OF MONARCHY HAS BEEN CUT OFF.
GO TO GEDALIAH, AND BE SAFE.
WAIT!
ONE OF YOUR PRISONERS -- I NEED TO SPEAK TO HIM.
DO AS YOU WILL.

THE LORD HAS SPOKEN TO ME OF YOU.
HE SAYS, "I AM ABOUT TO FULFILL MY WORDS AGAINST THIS CITY THROUGH DISASTER, NOT PROSPERITY. AT THAT TIME THEY WILL BE FULFILLED BEFORE YOUR EYES."
I THINK THAT'S FAIRLY OBVIOUS.
"BUT I WILL RESCUE YOU ON THAT DAY," DECLARES THE LORD; "YOU WILL NOT BE HANDED OVER TO THOSE YOU FEAR. I WILL SAVE YOU; YOU WILL NOT FALL BY THE SWORD BUT WILL ESCAPE WITH YOUR LIFE, BECAUSE YOU TRUST IN ME."
JEREMIAH, YOU DO KNOW THAT'S NOT WHY I HELPED YOU ...
YES, I DO. MORE IMPORTANTLY, SO DOES OUR LORD.
WHAT'S THAT YOU SAID?
I WAS JUST TELLING THIS MAN THAT THE LORD WILL PROTECT HIM ...
... FROM, WELL, FROM YOU.
AH.

LET THIS ONE GO AS WELL!

JEREMIAH?
I HAVE BEEN SET FREE.
IT HAPPENED, JUST AS THE LORD SAID ...
I STILL HELD OUT HOPE THAT IT WOULD NOT. NOW ... HOPE IS GONE.
YES, OUR CITY BURNS, JUST AS WE WERE TOLD.
BUT YOU MUST REMEMBER, THE CITY BURNS NOW ...
... BUT THERE IS STILL HOPE FOR TOMORROW.

"THERE IS ALWAYS HOPE FOR TOMORROW ..."